I Didn't Talk

Beatriz Bracher

I DIDN'T TALK

translated from the Portuguese
by Adam Morris

A NEW DIRECTIONS
PAPERBOOK ORIGINAL

Originally published in Brazil as *Não falei* by Editora 34.
Rights to this edition negotiated via literary agent Patricia Seibel
in association with Agência Riff.

New Directions gratefully acknowledges the Ministry of Culture /
National Library Foundation and the Ministry of Foreign Affairs of Brazil
for their support in the publication of this work.

MINISTÉRIO DAS RELACÕES EXTERIORES

MINISTÉRIO DA CULTURA
Fundação BIBLIOTECA NACIONAL

Grateful acknowledgment is made for permission to quote from "The Thaw"
by Primo Levi, translated by Ann Goldstein. Copyright © 2015 by Ann Goldstein.
Used by permission of Liveright Publishing Corporation.

Manufactured in the United States of America
New Directions Books are printed on acid-free paper
First published as a New Directions Paperbook (NDP 1413) in 2018
Design by Erik Rieselbach

Library of Congress Cataloging-in-Publication Data
Names: Bracher, Beatriz, author. | Morris, Adam J., translator.
Title: I didn't talk / by Beatriz Bracher ; translated by Adam Morris.
Other titles: Não falei. English
Description: New York : New Directions Publishing, 2018.
Identifiers: LCCN 2017055978 | ISBN 9780811227360 (alk. paper)
Subjects: LCSH: Urban violence—Brazil—Fiction. |
Brazil—Politics and government—20th century—Fiction. |
GSAFD: Political fiction
Classification: LCC PQ9698.412.R33 N3613 2018 | DDC 869.3/5—dc23
LC record available at https://lccn.loc.gov/2017055978

2 4 6 8 10 9 7 5 3 1

New Directions Books are published for James Laughlin
by New Directions Publishing Corporation
80 Eighth Avenue, New York 10011

I Didn't Talk

If it's possible to have a thought without a word or an image, without time and space—complete, created by me, a revelation of what remains hidden in me (and from me) but suddenly appears, if it could be born so clearly for all to see, without origin, without any effort of breath, of tone of voice, of rhythm or hesitation, without vision even, emerging like a normal thought, or more than a thought: a thing—if such a thing could exist, then I'd like to tell a story.

It happens every day. It's among strangers: that's where things emerge. It's how they become known. Stories are the shape we give things to pass the time on the bus, in line at the bank, at the bakery counter.

I asked, what do you do for a living? And he told me, I'm retired. Twenty years ago, at a motel café table, I found the answer unhelpful. His wife, all in white, looking like a nurse—an impression aided by her husband's physical disability—worked for the navy.

I was a school principal. Jobs help us make assumptions about people, the same as wrinkles on a face, the color of someone's skin, the clothes they wear, the way they butter their bread. "Retired" tells you nothing. A retired doctor, a retired garbage man, a retired president, a retired manicurist, yes, but not simply "retired." But today, yes, now I understand: *retired* is right.

Look, I was tortured, and they say I named a comrade who was later killed by soldiers' bullets. I didn't snitch—I almost died in the room where I could have snitched, but I didn't talk. They said I talked and Armando died. I was released two days after his death and they let me stay on as the school principal.

Eliana was in Paris. Our daughter, Lígia, was here, with my mother in this empty house, which back then was full. When I was imprisoned they arranged Eliana's trip to Paris. They didn't arrange for me to go anywhere. Eliana died. My father, sick and retired. My sister, Jussara, still a girl, was finishing school and doing a free prep course for her exams, studying all day. The family could never really count on José. Eliana died in Paris, she's buried there. After they released me, I talked to her on the phone. It was summer here, but she was trembling with cold, and complaining a lot about it—she wanted to see her daughter, bury her brother, take care of her mother—her voice trembled on the broken public phone she'd use to make free calls. I imagined her with purple lips, not dressed warmly enough. She couldn't come back—I knew she couldn't take it: she always felt the cold more than I did, but she couldn't come back, and that was all she had left.

Armando, my school friend, was her only brother. Luiza said that Eliana died of pneumonia without ever finding out that I'd said what I never said. I don't trust Luiza. How could someone die of pneumonia in Paris? She stopped eating. Yes, but weren't there friends around to feed and clothe her? I was furious. Luiza told me to remain strong for the revolution—

4

she hesitated, and her metallic voice took on the electricity of the military shocks, and to make things worse, I'd gone deaf in my right ear—no matter what happened to Armando you're still one of us, not everyone can take it, not even the strongest, Eliana died without knowing, don't worry. Dona Esther went crazy over the death of her son and daughter and wanted to hang on to her grandchild. I didn't go crazy but I couldn't touch Lígia. I found her baby talk intolerable.

Francisco Augusto, who'd recently left med school, reset the bones in my fingers, taping them to splints I tore off a week later, confirmed permanent deafness in my right ear, and recommended a dentist friend I should see about my two lost teeth. But I didn't go, and I didn't tell him about my nightmares or the impossibility of sleeping for more than fifteen minutes straight. We all have nightmares, and I couldn't go insane.

Dona Esther killed herself, but not without paying us one last visit, embracing Lígia, whispering in her granddaughter's ear a final goodbye mantra, and looking at me with disappointment: Armando trusted you even more than he trusted me.

At the café table in that provincial motel, the girl from the navy told us they were newlyweds. Eliana had been dead for ten years and I said, I'm a school principal, and the husband said "retired." I could have said biologist, or linguist, or educator. I had a full set of teeth again and was spending the holidays with Lígia and her friend Francisca, seeing the "historic cities" of Minas Gerais.

As though only some cities were historic. São Paulo's present history is so violent that it occupies space in possible pasts and futures: unable to look forward or backward or to the side, we stare down at our feet. When Lígia was ten, São Paulo still had the possibility of history and we'd go to the São Bento Monastery, the Pátio do Colégio, the Ipiranga Museum, the Consolação Cemetery. She could go by herself to buy bread at the bakery. She knew Dona Maria the grocer, Senhor Ademar the shoemaker, and she played with the neighborhood kids. I've been the victim of an urban bucolic that I don't like one bit. But my disbelief in the impossible is yielding: I'd rather not believe, and argue with Lígia about it. The move to São Carlos is the next phase in my career—I'm not giving up, as she alleges. I'm going to dedicate myself to Lucilia's project at the university, her study of language acquisition difficulties. Lígia thinks I should have taken the post at the Department of Education, or at least continued directing the program here in professional development and accepting requests for talks and seminars. But I'd like her to come with me. The university there is very good—her husband would have no trouble getting in and, more important, my little granddaughter Marta could go out by herself to buy our bread. Well, not yet, she's only three, but she'd come with me, and she'd get to know the baker, and the neighbors, and she'd pay attention to the color of the sky, the winds that bring the rain. No, I try to argue to myself, there's nothing bucolic here, in this empty house.

We finally sold the house. I have a few months left before I have to move out. I'm deciding which pieces of furniture are coming with me. José, Jussara, and Lígia took whatever they wanted after my mother's death. Jussara took only a few small things: some shirts, the oil painting of a little boy drawing, and the vanity mirror in its ugly mahogany frame, the kind so many houses had on Rua Teodoro Sampaio. It was Grandma Ana's and beloved by my mother—it was where she stuck little notes to remind herself of what she had to do the next day. Jussara grew up to be a beautiful, tall young woman, very thin like our father, but even so she took some of her short, plump mother's shirts, saying she'd wear them around the house, a house I've never visited: a respected psychiatrist, she raised her family in London and her children speak Portuguese with an accent. But she says she wears Dona Joana's clothes whenever she's home alone, especially a wool-gauze dressing gown that our mother often wore. I had to shrink Jussara a bit in my mind, imagine her littler, or else the gown was too short on her—too indecent to be something from Dona Joana's collection.

My mother was an excellent seamstress. She acquired important clientele, people from outside the neighborhood. "Important" was how she put it. And we knew who she meant, something that wouldn't make sense today. Now I wouldn't know how to place names or faces or occupations if someone said "important clientele." Obviously they weren't people from the neighborhood. When I went to elementary school, I had to take two buses and get off downtown, and I knew that being from outside the neighborhood wasn't enough to make someone important. Yet my mother treated all her customers the same, their clothes were all done with the same care, the prices fixed. The importance of the customer was only apparent in the quality of the cloth and my mother's patience. The important ones—my mother would say as she prepared dinner at the stove, as José and I did our homework, and Jussara, the baby, ten years younger than José, slept in her crib—are the most distrustful. They're afraid I don't know the names of the cuts, so they explain every little detail. My mother found this lack of trust reasonable enough: shoddy workmanship is rampant everywhere—ignorance has no fixed address, no mark on its forehead. She'd listen attentively and humbly repeat the details. It's just, she'd say, that some of the important customers use the terms incorrectly: they want a ruffled skirt but they say pleated, they want a three-quarter-length sleeve and they say half sleeve. You can't correct them, mainly because it doesn't get you anywhere, so mistaken but so assured, poor things, and so I have to show them with fabric how it will look, find a photo of a similar model. Only then can I know for sure what they want. You have to understand that these people have never had the opportunity to *learn*.

The late Dona Joana was a very intelligent but unambitious person. She regarded both stupidity and ambition as birth defects or traits acquired through life's mishaps, and felt it was necessary to be as patient with such people as with the blind and the deaf.

Armando liked Dona Joana. We were classmates in elementary school and again in high school. In the weeks leading up to our exams, he'd come have lunch with me and we'd study together until late afternoon. Francisco Augusto was Armando's classmate in med school. He's a good doctor, just as Armando no doubt would have been. I studied biology, then education, and then linguistics. Now I'm going to São Carlos. Armando used to talk to my mother. About recipes, seasonings, or little things about the city and its characters. Some dishes were renamed "Armando's." We'd had them all before: pasta with meatballs, sautéed squash, baked rice without olives but with fresh corn, toast with creamed spinach and minced hard-boiled egg. Only now they were Armando's meatballs, Armando's rice, the same old thing, but under new management. José, Jussara, our father, and I—we didn't have dishes named after us, although we ate them with pleasure. I think that Armando's sort of praise wasn't part of our language—maybe that's what it was. Sometimes I got caught up with something downtown and stayed there, annoying Armando. He didn't want to miss out on Dona Joana's food so he learned how to get there by himself and would go on his own. He'd say he could only study properly while listening to the *tac-tac* of the sewing machine.

I'm healthy, the illnesses I get come and go without medication, I cost very little. My mother and father are dead. Jussara has taken care of herself for decades now, Lígia and her husband have found their footing, Renato is no more, and so with my pension I have more than I need. I don't have a car with registration or taxes, no microwave or any other useless machine, only a computer that crashes every so often, requiring me to call the ever-stranger Alexandre, the grandson of my ancient neighbor, Dona Eulália, who comes over and futzes with it and forgets to charge me. The house, which is old, needs constant work: a burst pipe, burned-out wiring, a door that squeaks but won't shut anymore. It's all going to hell, so I have an agreement with Tobias, a thrifty handyman. He tells me gently the house needs a complete overhaul, the pipes have to be replaced, the wiring requires this and that and who knows what else. But I've bravely resisted for these past thirty years, ever since I got out of prison, ever since Eliana died and I moved back here. I always had my father's firm support, but after he died I had to keep up the fight alone. Lígia, Jussara, and my mother all took Tobias's side and wanted the renovation, the overhaul, changing everything, but my side prevailed and the house was allowed to age in peace. Now a developer will tear it down, like all the other old homes around us, and many families will live off this sale, including Lígia's: I put my share toward an apartment for her and there was still enough left over for a small house with a yard in São Carlos.

José was here a few days ago, he slept three nights in our old bedroom. I sleep in our parents' old room. He came to speak with his editor and with people from the newspaper and the magazines he writes for. He saved the last night for us to eat dinner together. That was how he put it: I left Friday free for us to have dinner, you have any plans? Aside from sleeping, no sir, I replied, like I was reporting to one of the important clients. He found this funny—he knows I'm too lazy to go out at night and the farmers' hours I keep. We barely saw each other on Wednesday and Thursday. He has his own key and knows where to find sheets and towels, and despite his criticisms he makes do with my jam-jar glasses, my mismatched plates and bent silverware. It's the last month of the professional development courses for teachers, and I still needed to show up for meetings to prep for next semester and to attend the commencement ceremonies. Goodbyes were said, and homage paid, as if I were leaving for another planet where wizened São Paulistanos, having forsaken its flux, are put out to pasture. The past tense triumphed in each tribute, and I left more irritated than when I arrived. Being buried alive annoyed me. It was such an efficient, elegant way to stop listening to what I have to say, or reading with glazed eyes what I write. How can we be giving courses in professional development when we're the ones who need to be brought up to speed? I no longer believe in any of this. *But Professor*— that awful little voice of respect that I can't stand—*it's what's possible*. I think I got tired of possibility, it doesn't interest me anymore. Anyway I'm finishing something off with this move: it's certainly an ending. I am killing something, I don't know exactly what, maybe ambition, since even Dona Joana couldn't keep the mishaps of life from infecting me with that too.

I went to the university early on Friday to clear out my office, submit grades for all the stragglers, sign off on all the necessary bureaucratic things to formally free myself, and have lunch with Teresa. Early that morning, as I was putting the bread and newspaper on the kitchen table with an automatic gesture whose predicate is to turn toward the stove, take a pot, fill it with water, set it to boil, et cetera, I gave a start—the bread and the newspaper nearly broke two teacups, two saucers, and two small plates from the old china set José took after our mother died, which were now set out neatly with white napkins. There was also a vase with flowers and a gift, wrapped in gold paper, with a note from my brother. My first reaction was to look around to make certain I wasn't in the wrong house. Then, irritation with this invasion of my breakfast ritual—my coffee in a glass, sweetened coffee in the pot, my baguette with butter and crumbs on the old table. In the rage and confusion of these last days, as everyone around me was calling them, I pushed it all aside, took out my cup, pulled apart my bread, and read my newspaper—starting with the sports section, an old habit of Armando's that had grown on me the past few years, as though I'd always done it. I threw my brother's gift on my bed and took his note with me to read on the bus to the university.

Mine, mine, mine. Like a little child learning the tribe's tongue, I find myself in the acquisitive phase of a new language. At the same time the old phrases, the ones I knew and used, seem to have become sterile—transformed beyond recognition. Now it was *my* cup, *my* bread, *my* rage, *my* sixty-four years of age—as if I needed once more to name and claim what I was taking with me. Return to the first person and to the possessive, modernity's twin juvenile plagues, against which I'd always struggled so sincerely. José's note spoke of the same necessity—but in a diametrically opposite way. He wrote of reminiscing and I think of creating; he wrote of discovering and I need to be establishing. Yet his note brought me peace, banishing the childish indignation that in recent days had left me too restless to think—frivolous, vibrating, orphaned and prone to pure reaction. His Machadian tone—which José cultivates in a way that borders on plagiarism yet somehow remains, paradoxically, his own—revived my happiness in the same way that, when absorbed in something specific and complex, we're surprised by birdsong. Maybe the bird had been singing for a while, maybe its song had been softly penetrating the machinations of logic. But we perceive it suddenly, as if it had been born alongside our unexpected joy at hearing it. The song pulls us out of ourselves, obliterates the train of thought we'd been following, leaves us only the pleasure of listening to the bird. Often, when we realize we're happy—and have lost our train of thought—we sigh, resigned to the idea of starting over again, when the solution appears as clearly and as unexpectedly as the birdsong. As José wrote, "*This is what happens to me, as I go about remembering and shaping the construction or reconstruction of myself*" (Machado, as written by José).

As I go about remembering, what a beautiful thing. I need to reread Machado, and retrieve the unexpected things I no longer remember. Unlike José—who, as he searches, tries like Dom Casmurro to construct a past that will be kind to him in the present—I seek my errors, I kick stones and send the cockroaches scurrying, I walk my face through spiderwebs and ask of every smug milestone I've passed, what purpose did you serve in my life? Did you manage to hold firm, or emit light, or make noise, or at least serve as a pillar, to sustain whoever reached you? Or—already so eaten away by applause—could the flick of a finger tumble you over a cliff and into the calm and muddy river of the satisfied?

Inside the gold package on my bed was José's new book, the first volume, I'd read in the note, of an autobiographical cycle. It was an advance copy and he wanted my opinion. Although artfully written, the request was sincere; it moved me, even if I couldn't help but find it amusing. José had already exposed himself and our family in his very first book, his most experimental and the one I like best. None of them is straightforwardly bad—they all have charm and depth. But for all the genres he's tried—detective stories, historical fiction, critical essays—there's something predictable that I find off-putting. I know where he wants to end up (he provides, in fact, long explanations, in which his sexuality plays an increasingly important role). But his note moved me: it's my brother's first direct request in many years. Even in his most dire straits, he never asked us for anything, never let down his guard for us so we could help him. He moved away a long time ago. He was a hippie in Arembepe, saw a flying saucer somewhere over the Planalto Central, went backpacking in Machu Picchu, got stoned in California until—with the sudden conversion of a hold-out—José became an academic, a man of letters. He got a fellowship in Germany, then one in Spain, and finally returned to live in Curitiba. After our father's death he came to visit more frequently. When our mother got sick, five years ago, he moved back home and, for the two months before she died, he cared for her. You couldn't call it a reconciliation, because there'd never been a fight. *Reencounter* is the right word, from José's point of view.

I, on the other hand, lived my whole life with Dona Joana. I could never reencounter her. And the truth is our mother could never reencounter José either. Since he'd left home at

seventeen, her son had gone through so many transforma-
tions, all so far beyond her ken, that her affection for the ma-
ture man was more of the kind you might feel for the friend
of your dead son—one who reminds you, with his presence,
his age, and his stories, of the boy who passed away and no
longer exists. "The teacups," the note continued, "are part
of the set we used to use when we were little, and which I
took when we split up her things. I thought of all the reasons
they're so special to me and why I want to share with you, my
older brother, reuniting something that time divided, but all
my reasons, no matter how sincere would only annoy you.
We've never spoken about keepsakes, but I can imagine your
opinion—I'm aware of your aversion to junk and of your pref-
erence for coffee in a jar. I only ask that you accept them, with
my sincere affection."

I agreed to have lunch with Teresa because I enjoy her com-
pany, a feeling I think is mutual and which allows us to share
an understanding, stimulating even when it comes to discussing academic concerns. This time there were no concerns, just
an end-of-the-year lunch for two. We agreed to meet in the
department café and then go somewhere nearby so we could
have a decent meal, with some peace and quiet. She was with a
young woman who looked like one of my undergrads. I don't
remember much about her, only that she was charming—but
then there are so many—and I can't recall her name, Ercília
or Marília, or something like that. It turned out she's writing
a novel set in the Sixties and Seventies, and she wanted to interview me. She'd already interviewed several people when
Teresa had suggested me. Her protagonist was more or less my
age, had been imprisoned, became an educator. She needed
information about the period, about the education system—
details of daily life in the schools and in prison. She said she'd

already read my books. I think she was studying pedagogy or anthropology, I didn't quite catch that. She hadn't known that I'd been a prisoner, had participated in the movement. I didn't participate, I said. But Teresa made a pouty face, as if I were being difficult or modest. I didn't want to upset Teresa, but the situation really bothered me. Sensing this, the girl was intimidated. She's interesting, this girl. I mean—well, I mean, no, that's just it, she's serious, pretty, and this wasn't mere idle curiosity. Finally Teresa asked her to say more about her book. The girl said she'd just started working at a public school and was taken aback by the "aggressive emptiness" she felt between the teachers. In the novel she wanted to portray a time when education still seemed to have a more explosive meaning, a detonating force—and where this had eventually led. She'd already read books about the history of education, and about the repression of the resistance movements. She'd seen the films and heard the songs, but she said she needed to interview people because her book wasn't about politics or education, but about something she wasn't quite certain she fully understood yet. Now that I think about it, she's pretty bold, this girl. I knew exactly what she was talking about, because I'd thought about all this plenty of times myself—but I don't like being the raw material that somebody else sucks dry.

At the time however I found it charming, this shameless inquiry into my life, so transparent, utilitarian. She said she needed to know the slang from that period, nuances and details that you can't get from reading books. She admired my ideas, that I understood, but ideas weren't what she wanted—none of that mattered. She wanted my *age*. To ferret out words from those years that still lingered in the speech of older men. A Trojan Horse, this gift from Teresa. Now I can't get it out of my head, this girl and her interview. She even ended up with my phone number, though she hasn't called yet. I hope she doesn't call. It's a bad time. I told her I hardly remembered anything and she said she wanted that too—the broken memories, the scrambled view of what remained—everything that was vanishing into the aggressive void.

She said she'd like to read some of my more recent work before conducting her interview, and Teresa mentioned the reports and letters I'd sent not long ago to the Department of Education, offering my unsolicited opinions regarding the latest direction teaching had taken. I ended up telling the girl I'd send them to her, even though they weren't public documents. What was her name? Josefina? Maria? There's no way I'd call Teresa to ask. When the girl calls, she'll say her name. It's no good, this business of forgetting even recent things. I jotted down her email someplace, but I think it was only her initials. I'd written it down so I'd remember to send her the letters and reports, but I haven't had the time.

I'm disorganized and forgetful, which is why I created a rather rigid methodology, external to me, from which I wouldn't be able to escape. I became what appears to be a punctual, organized, and responsible person. *Appears* is the right word, but without its insinuation of falsehood, which is connected and consecutive to superficial, incomplete knowledge. He appears to be generous, but once you really get to know him—you can't even imagine. This would actually be a good way to teach Portuguese. Take an expression at random, one that arises in a trivial classroom conversation, when we're not—when we *appear* not to be—teaching. In those innumerable instants when the teacher speaks about a spouse or against the government, or when a student—but trivial conversation rarely comes from the students. In those moments we can interrupt ourselves to call attention to the word being used. That's the birdsong. Or the appearance of a priest in a church when we're only there to see the stained-glass windows. That moment in which we perceive another dimension of what we're doing, the object we're examining, the instruments we're using. The value of error: this is precisely the value of error. Yes, because the birdsong in the middle of muddling through Kant is certainly an error, as much as when the flesh-and-blood priest appears right beside you as you're going on about the Baroque. Error skewers our thought, distracting us. And such is the magic of errors: we return from them changed. Like an errant trajectory, suddenly on the wrong street—only then do we stop to think about the general design of streets and their layout and choose the most interesting path, which may or may not be the shortest. And so the teacher uses the word *apparently* in an unusual way, stops and says, how curious, we sometimes use "appear" to say that something is false, that it seems to be something that in reality it isn't. But when you think about it, we also use it to say that something appears to us in such a way, in such a form, and that's the only way we know it—the way in which something appears. Because we aren't sure if it will remain, over time, the same way we see it now. Or perhaps we suspect it will be able to change, so we say that it now appears as such. But when we say that something *appears*, do we really mean that it's false? Or do we only use it to express our hesitation, which may not be motivated in any way by the thing in itself? And then we can open the dictionary together with the students to find out if *apparent* has any relation to *parent*.

I always favored the presence, in every classroom, of a Portuguese dictionary, an etymological dictionary, a Latin dictionary, a Greek dictionary, a common grammar, and a dictionary of verb and prepositional correspondences. And not in some corner of the room, but on my desk, to be handled at all times, without formality.

I say I appear organized because that is how I've become in relation to the world, without having changed my nature. Thus: *apparently*. I am organized to everyone who comes into contact with me and only to myself *apparently* organized. But I didn't send those report letters to that girl of Teresa's. Not because I lack discipline, or because she doesn't deserve my help. I left it to the end of the week to decide what I'd send her, and ever since, I've been hesitating. The dinner with José came in between.

Eliana died at twenty-five. Tomorrow she'd be fifty-nine. I don't think there was a suicidal vein in the family—Dona Esther's melancholy was more Lusitanian than depressive. She was widowed young, with small children, and sold her father-in-law's bakery (which her bohemian husband had inherited and never knew what to do with). She bought two houses to rent out for income and went to work for a Catholic association for women. As Dona Joana would say, she had the opportunity to learn, and learn she did. When I was young, I was envious of Armando, of his mother who worked away from home, of his father's absence; he had the family apartment to himself and all the responsibilities of the man of the house. In comparison to our little clan huddled under Dona Joana's wings and my father's black umbrella, it all seemed modern and adult. When I first met him, Armando would get his sister from her school every evening at five. I never heard him complain the way I did on the few occasions my mother asked me to watch Jussara. He didn't regard what he did for his mother as a favor; it was one of his household duties, like going to the bank to pay the bills. The house was an apartment and it was his: he had a set of keys, his mother consulted him on the best way to manage their domestic budget. In my house Dona Joana left no space for any of us to assume such a role.

Compared with José, I appeared to be a very independent young man, an appearance that my contact with Armando cracked open to reveal a mama's boy—that was a bitch, but nothing could be done about it. When I looked after Jussara so my mother could go out, or when I brought her some kind of fastening from the notions store downtown, on my way home from school, she'd tousle my hair, the smile on her face expressing pride in her little boy, all grown up. It was so different from the way Dona Esther treated Armando when he gave her the receipts from the bills he'd paid at the bank, along with her change. She didn't thank him. She sighed, remarked on how costly life was, she praised God that she had a job and, unlike the women she served in the institution where she worked, she didn't depend on others for help. The scholarship that Eliana had received to study in the Catholic school hurt her pride, and she and Armando decided that the way to set things right would be for Eliana to attend the same public high school that we did, and by then she'd be old enough to catch the bus by herself and make her own lunch.

Eliana, who would be fifty-nine years old tomorrow, was passionately devoted to her brother. Armando—a loud-mouth, a truant who always got away with things, a ringleader, a prankster, a mediocre soccer center striker, a mediator of various factions, a spokesman for all our student demands, a merrymaker, a glutton, a foul mouth, and a miser—felt part of any group that life set before him, claiming the role of brother or father no matter where you put him. Eliana on the other hand belonged to only one group, her family triad: a chosen people, bearers of the mark. It was necessary to deserve it, the mark, which she daily mastered through her dedication to her studies and how seriously she measured her thoughts and actions. Francisco Augusto says that love triangles hold more love than duets. He says that the desire to defeat and dominate is what preserves love. Eliana was possessed by the obligation to serve and to live up to a certain standard. She couldn't fail. Up to the standard of her mother, first of all, and then, forever and always, her brother. She wasn't timid, submissive, or defensive—she was delicate. She had that joy of the very serious. She died without knowing, Luiza said, don't worry.

I'm hesitating not because I'm afraid to expose my incoherence. Retired, said the man who moved with the help of a walker and his new wife. I'm in the navy, said the wife in white, and we're newlyweds. Apparently we don't know anything about the people we see and when they tell us what they are—retired, in the navy—we're surprised because without realizing it, we already knew the entirety of their lives: something inside us has woven their stories. Mainly about the things they don't tell us. In the bakery, that pretty girl with the bags under her eyes, I think: she's married, she's nursing and doesn't sleep much at night. She proudly displays her weariness and the leaked-milk stain on her low-cut dress. She has the voice of a queen and her gaze is distracted; she loves and is loved and the love flows into the bread, the butter, the milk, the baker, and transforms even the famished gaze of the little urchin upon her breast into an homage to maternity—and this is how we make people known and familiar, enclosed in a story that doesn't threaten us. When the girl in white at the motel said, I'm in the navy, she guided my thoughts, charting a fixed course—that of the nurse who'd used her husband's infirmity to make herself indispensable and loved, yet with a love always threatened by the possibility that her companion might be cured. I don't know whether this information about her was enriching or limiting.

Life is full of surprises. I'm in the navy, said the girl in white. This cancer, it's already taken my breasts and given me these silicone tits, said the girl from the bakery, it's eating me from the inside and I want life, bread, the baker, and the hunger of this little boy. The danger, when confronted by these surprises, is to say to ourselves, oh yes, now I understand, and to halt the process of imagination, deactivating it. To accept navy and cancer, archiving them in pigeonholes called soldier and death, is to discard, as error, care and maternity.

Oh, how thought betrays. Next to error, betrayal is my engine. I was going to talk about two beautiful women who attracted me, as if I meant nothing by it, only to illustrate a prosaic analogy, and I've returned to soldiers and death. Soldiers and death. Where along the way did I lose the shining, dark skin of my domineering navy nurse and the pulsing tenderness of my new mother? Soldiers and death. Left-right, left-right, march little solider, in your soft beret. The trick is to accept these betrayals of reality and thought—incite them, remain open to receive them—but never submit to them.

The letters and reports I wrote to the Department of Education, criticizing where trends are heading and the evaluations designed by the current government—they'd be interesting for that girl of Teresa's, so objective, so emphatic, up to date, and above all, rather specific. The center of that void that perturbs her. I'm not considering publishing them, but it might be productive to show them to her. A reading of the letters would bring out contradictions of certain things I've written in my books, which is interesting. It might deconstruct the image she's made of me, of my thoughts. Or it might reinforce what I always say about the necessity of self-subversion. Something more than just an old man, I still feel the strength and desire to err and to betray and to strike my target. Not strength for defending what I've already said, that's foolish, but strength for thinking anew—but will I? Right about now I'm tired and confused, almost disinterested. I think about the girl and her curiosity, but her topic doesn't excite me. Still, the letters are a moment of vigor and struggle. Why do I hesitate?

By Friday's dinner, I hadn't yet started to read the manuscript of José's new book. He was emotional, saying goodbye to the house, taking Polaroids of every corner, and regretting having ever agreed to the sale.

—What do you mean, agree? You and Jussara had to convince me to sell it.

—No, no, I don't want to argue, I'm not criticizing you. Jussara needed the money, and I thought you did, too, now that you're retiring.

—José, please. I'm moving to São Carlos because we're selling the house, not the other way around, so spare me your good intentions.

—Calm down, professor, no need to shout.

—I'm not shouting, I'm emphasizing.

—It's all fine, it was an attractive offer and ever since she died I've never wanted to come back, it brings me down. But I didn't realize your attachment was so strong and besides, my life has been a never-ending process of leaving things behind, going away, burning bridges, and starting over with a few more scars. You know I burn all my originals and proofs? I keep no kind of diary, no record, no notes. I've always been that way. But now that I've begun to write about our childhood, I feel the lack.

—Our childhood, José, *ours*?

—Yes, that's what brothers tend to have in common, their childhoods. You can't change that, can't destroy it.

—What do you mean, destroy?

José cooked dinner: the spaghetti Bolognese of our childhood, with sauce, diced onion and tomato, and lightly browned ground beef. Eating calmed us down. I complimented the dish and he told me about life in Curitiba. His project—our childhood, myself though his eyes—was a latent theme.

—So, when will you move to São Carlos?

—The demolition crew starts work at the beginning of March but I want to be in São Carlos by the first week in February. Lucilia wants me to move now, right after Christmas. But I don't want to stay at her place and the painters will only be finished at the end of January. I'll move as soon as it's ready.

—If we hadn't sold the house, would you have stayed here?

—I don't know. Now that it's said and done, I think it's for the best, and that I should have left São Paulo a long time ago. But there was always the house.

—Really, I didn't know it was so important to you, it didn't even occur to me.

—It's nothing like that, José, it was laziness, the path of least resistance. But as soon I was forced to move on, to make a new home, my old idea of working with Lucilia came back to me—I'm not leaving São Paulo so much as getting out of the university environment—working only on linguistics, returning to my research without the burden of administering this or negotiating that.

—You'll see how nice it is to get out of São Paulo and leave behind the stress, the violence. A peaceful environment will help you pay more attention to yourself.

—That's exactly what I don't want, José, to think about myself. I'm not leaving because of the violence, but to escape the stagnation of only thinking. Violence is at least some kind of action.

José asked if he could move in after I left, so that he could take advantage of the last weeks of its ghosts, incarnate in bricks, switches, doorknobs, the change in light in between the kitchen and the living room, the echo of footfalls on the last stair, the squeak in the floorboards outside our room, which continues all the way to our parents' room. One last, long night without mother's kiss.

The good sort of ghosts, professor. Tortured, but good. Imagine that one day you're walking down the street, returning from campus, tired, no, not tired, distracted, recalling things that happened throughout the day, without bothering to organize your thoughts, just letting them wash over you, leaving behind diffuse impressions, feelings, a chill, a shiver, a surprise—but at what, you can't really say. And while lost in thought you drift past your regular bus stop and decide to get on later, so as not to interrupt the flow of memory. You stop on a corner to wait for the light. Before you realize it, it's already changed and then switched back again. You look around to see where you are and beside you a boy signals for you to follow him. He doesn't gesture, doesn't say anything, but you know that he's summoning you. You divert your eyes and the image of the boy remains. You don't know who he is, you're certain you've never seen him before. But at the same time he's familiar—too familiar, you might say. You watch him from the corner of your eye, not wanting to meet his gaze. He's standing there, waiting for the light to change. He's just a normal boy, waiting for the light, he's not looking at you but he's still summoning. The light changes and then changes back and the two of you still stand there waiting. Who is he? A student from years ago? A friend's son? No: you know you've never seen him, and yet he's completely familiar, almost just like you. The light changes and you both cross the street, proceeding down the same sidewalk. It's your way home. You've never walked this way, you always do this stretch by bus, you've been commuting that way for years. From up in the bus you've seen the houses, the pedestrians. Maybe that's it, maybe he always walks this way at the same time you go past on the bus, and you've seen him from above. His gait and his clothes are both unremarkable. Why should he draw your attention to the point of recognition? Because it's been so many years, looking and looking, and maybe he's become fixed in your memory without you having realized it. But no, he couldn't be more than twenty or so, and people don't look the same way for long at that age. Now he stops and fishes in his pocket, and with a key in his hand he turns toward the twin row house. Yes, of course, the twin row house. The kind born in pairs, identical twins. The difference of a split, the division of a whole—when we speak of a part, we indicate that a whole exists, but a part has no individual existence without the whole. A twin row house, a twin, they're individuals, they're whole, but they carry another in their name. Yes, you've thought this many times while staring at the twin row house, standing there between two other buildings, I was a twin, but my brother was stillborn.

(José went out of his way to find my fury, my fate, my mark of Cain.)

If one of the houses were demolished, destroyed, the other would still remain half of a twin row house: it's written into the architecture, its roof slopes only on one side. Its entire symmetry demands the other side, already undone. I can't stop myself from being a twin, not a part, but an individual who carries in his structure another, nonexistent.

You thought about what never existed for us, only for you, and of what came before your time, you now remember having such thoughts at times, you were refining your thoughts, but only when you passed that stretch of the street. On the next corner there's a pastry shop that you now regret you never tried, never remembered to skip the bus and walk to the pastry shop, get a chocolate eclair for Jussara, some meringues for mother, a donut for Lígia. This is an old memory, Ju still in medical school, mother where she always was, alive, and Lígia a little girl, playing on the floor with grandma's rag dolls. But then another thing caught your attention. There were days when, distracted, you didn't notice the house. Did you feel its lack? A window left open before going out can gnaw at you before you can put your finger on what's bothering you. I think that without being able to put your finger on it, you didn't know it was the house that you missed—even though in recent days you surprised yourself by waiting for it to appear. You fixed your attention on the difference between the two equals. Both old, something becoming to a house, both with the same door made of thick wood, blinds in the upper windows, the little verandah made of spaced red bricks, the low wall in front adorned with yellow stones, separating the little yard from the street, and the white iron gate, the same moulding on the doors and windows. But it was only when the bus got stuck in traffic that you could tell they were identical, even if each was its own.

The one of the left, where the boy was now turning his key, is reasonably well kept: no embellishments, never a new color, the paint flaking in a few places, the red bricks blackened, the garden in front showing signs of ownership. From the bus you can't see the debris on the ground, only the roses, always in bloom. The one on the right-hand side is graffitied, the slats in the blinds are missing or bent, the gate is shut with rusted wire, the grass grows wild, and a thriving vine, perhaps a bougainvillea that doesn't bloom, a male, has pulled shingles off the house. You always observed the one on the left. You'd noticed that it was a twin row house but your gaze never apprehended its pair, the *one on the right, in spite of having perceived the harmony of the composition. What if I went to live there? No. There's our mother, Jussara, Lígia. No. But what if I lived here in addition to there—an office, something simple, for receiving students, colleagues, a study group, a place to bring a girlfriend, a place that didn't talk except to me, or that wouldn't say so much about me. Oh, the pastry shop, I forgot again.*

On the day of the traffic jam your thoughts apprehended the house on the right, the identity and the difference, it named them the living and the dead. Strange, the way we attribute to death this stagnation, and to life this flow. And time flowed more visibly for the dead house than the living one. In our bodies, as well. If Renato were alive,

(I would have raised an eyebrow at this point, when José switched from one death to another)

or Eliana, or our father—if our father were alive his body would be recognizable, whereas now, underground. . . .

Anyway, the boy goes inside, the door doesn't groan the way you remember thinking it would. It frightened you not to hear it creak, it was so familiar, and you hadn't even realized it, this familiarity you developed with the house. The door to the house on the left was on its right, near to the division with its pair. But strangely, when the boy opens the door and leaves it ajar, waiting for you to follow, you see a light coming from inside to the right, where there ought to be a dividing wall, the border. A very strong light, filtered by the opaque texture of a lampshade, reflected on dark woods and the spines of old books. Its power didn't derive from intensity, but from revelation. You enter. The light from the right side absorbs you. You aren't entering the house of a stranger, the light belongs to you.

No resistance or willpower or curiosity moved you, it took no effort to climb the stairs, cross the verandah, and step over the threshold of those houses. They weren't one, but they were connected as if they were. The source of the light sucked you to the right, like a small child pulling his father by the hand, closer to the magician he fears and yet still wants to watch—and the father, rooted to the ground, continues talking to a friend, or finishes paying for cotton candy and waits for his change. Just like that you were brought to a halt before you crossed the second threshold, with your feet already turned to the right, in the direction of the light, your body turned to the left, and you discerned in a single glance the apartment where you and Eliana had made a home together,

(where is this going, José?)

the furniture, the layout, the tonality of the air, the way it carried the sound of Eliana's voice, the armchair where Armando would sit when he visited, the cushion he crushed under his arm, it was there, crushed,

(we didn't have an armchair, just a chintzy sofa that ended up who knows where)

the double bed, a present from Dona Esther,

(that got sold)

and Dona Joana's curtains in the kitchen window

(no, no, we only had an ugly, narrow ventilation window in our tiny, hot kitchen)

you're standing there, half-turned, your feet pointed one way and your eyes glancing back, you want to move in the direction of the light but you're waiting for something, and a murmur resonates, the memory of Eliana's voice, not her voice, but her slow cadence, her serious tone—they're in the air,

(I hear Eliana clearly. It doesn't scare me when, in bed, her voice calls out to me.)

you try to understand fragments of words, meanings that might still be found in those tattered sounds that resound around the old apartment.

The light finally gets you moving, you turn toward the house on the right and step into an enormous library, long and oval, vaulted ceilings, the whole space lit by a small lamp with a shade made of human skin.

(José, please)

The lamp is small and the light looks darker inside the shade than out. The skin intensifies the light. Your myopic eyes can clearly read the spines of all the books and for some reason that doesn't alarm you; you can even read the inside of each book you pass. All the authors that you ever read or wanted to read are there, as well as books unwritten and others long since disappeared. The words, sentences, and paragraphs that your eyes graze: together they conjure the feelings you had when you read them for the first time. The joys of discovery return to you intact. The words, which had already been transformed in you, returned to their original authors, their brothers, this family that constitutes you, each one of your bones, your nerves, the story of your skin and the movement of your guts, you hear all the words, you drift along tense threads of pleasure, your manhood getting larger, aching beneath your pants; it's extremely hard. You ejaculate.

You open your eyes to the sound of the key turning in the lock. You're stopped on the pavement in front of the house. The boy comes out to face the imbecile at the gate. His eyes like mulberries, organic and endless—it's difficult to face them but you can't avoid them, his eyes, your eyes, brother, they burn, as though you can't blink. The boy moves toward you, crosses the verandah, descends the stairs, touches the gate, and you're stuck there, unable to avert your gaze. The boy smiles: he has good manners for dealing with a lost old man. Good afternoon, sir, can I help you with something? His voice doesn't have anything special to it, and when he smiles the prison of his gaze falls away. You're free, you don't respond, you turn and go on your way, once again forgetting to visit the pastry shop.

José—*recent exchange*

Look, José, I told him, you don't need the house or the ghosts that inhabit it. Not even the ones you think belong to me. Anyway, the house is yours, and I'm not just trying to be kind or fulfill some obligation—come whenever you like. Maybe he'll come by after the New Year. I'll try to hurry up with my move.

Yesterday I went to the cemetery. I like old cemeteries, the chapels and mausoleums, the letters they use on the grave plaques, the epitaphs. I like the dates in particular. I lamented that Eliana wasn't here, in São Paulo. Her name and her dates. When Lígia was little, we used to go for walks in the city cemeteries. She liked the one on Dr. Arnaldo Avenue the best. Maybe it was the row of flower stands, but I think it was mostly for its narrow little streets lined with monuments rising up the hill, like houses. Sunday is always a nice day for cemeteries: more people are out, and in general the world is much calmer. Lanes for strolling slowly, where strangers greet one another, where you can stop and be still and quiet without causing alarm. Lígia would run, spinning round and round, and play within a radius of me that she considered safe. We'd buy flowers at the entrance and she'd place them, one by one, into the little vases on the graves she liked best, like the breadcrumbs we fed to the fish in the park one Sunday. Lígia imitated the gestures of the older ladies standing before certain graves, kneeling and murmuring with her hands brought together near her mouth. My daughter had it down, the way those murmurs were like little kisses the women gave their hands: she did the same, sometimes with devotion—her eyes closed, her brow creased—other times just for fun. One day I saw her standing in front of a grave looking very serious, her posture erect, her hands clasped behind her, her head bowed low over her chest. Watching from afar, I saw that she was imitating a tall and elegant man who was meditating before a tomb. The man then threw his head back, let out a long sigh, crossed his arms over his chest, and let his gaze wander across the sky. After a while he clapped his hands together, just once, rubbed them against each other, and went on his way, amusing himself by reading the inscriptions along his path. Lígia repeated his movements and I found it funny. From then on she conducted the ritual she'd learned from the tall man for the graves she considered the most important. For the humbler ones, the ones without a chapel or a statue, she performed the old-lady routine: she would kneel, kiss her hands, and get up again as though they were steps in a dance. The tall man's clap, which he had done only once to mark the end of a thought, became applause. Dances, kisses, claps: the homage my daughter paid to the dead. Maybe in a park I wouldn't be able to tolerate our daughter's levity, but on hallowed ground her laughter couldn't wound me.

And then there were the stories. She would ask me to read the dates, the names. We'd figure out how old people were when they died and then make up their life stories. Lígia wanted me to look for children. She imagined them to be like herself and her classmates. Maybe he was playing on top of a wall and fell off? Maybe a bad wolf ate him? Or he drank tainted water from the faucet? With old people, her imagination ran along the lines of her grandmother and her grandmother's friends, especially Dona Josefa, a neighbor whose arms were spotted, dry, and wrinkled—something Lígia always noticed. The old ones were always kindly, they gave presents to their grandchildren, told them stories, drank water slowly, but they kept getting older and older and older, so old that they couldn't hear any longer, couldn't see—they hunched over, turned into frogs, and died. I pointed to people who came to visit their graves and told her they were probably relatives who looked like the dead. But Lígia preferred her own versions.

One day she asked to see her mother's grave. I explained that it was far away. But why? Because she died far away. But why can't her grave be here? I'd told her that tombs were monuments that people make for loved ones who have died. It was a way of feeling closer to them: when we read their names and dates, we remember their lives and how nice it was to be their friend. Like a photograph, but better, because they always stay in the same place, where anybody can pass by and read the names and dates and remember nice things about them. But I hadn't said the obvious: that their bodies are buried beneath the markers. I could sense that Lígia didn't know. How could she? Two self-conceptions struggled inside me: that of the *educator*, in the sense of he who protects and nurtures, and that of the *traitor*, he who hands something over, transmits knowledge. But what kind of knowledge was this anyway? The putrefied cadaver of the mother she'd never known? Selfishness won out: I wished to conserve for what little time I could my happy ballerina for the dead. Dancing for the memory of the dead. I said, it's true, you're right, we'll find your mother's grave. The next Sunday I took a box of colored chalk and wrote Eliana's name and dates on the grave under which Armando, Dona Esther, and my father-in-law, Dom Estevão, lay buried. Lígia drew little flowers and hearts. On our next visit, the name was already washed off, so we decided to write it again with a piece of metal, etching it into the stone, *Eliana Bastos Ferreira, 1945–1970*. I was happy with our work, almost cheerful: child's play, a foolish thing, and there was Eliana, with us.

Once, when Lígia was five or six years old, she brought a friend home. I proposed that we visit a museum or a park. I suggested Butantã, but Lígia wanted to show the cemetery to Francisca, who was excited to see it. I could tell it was something they'd been discussing for a while. Later, at the entrance, each one with her flowers, they took off running. Lígia stopped in front of certain graves and told her friend stories that I'd never heard. Princesses, Japanese ladies, and witches. The cemetery was her first library: each tomb a tome. The stories always ended with someone flying through the sky. And then she died and turned into a bird-person and flew away. Her mommy and daddy got sad, because regular people can't feed bird-people, they can't take them to school or put them to bed because they fly away and leave them. So they make graves for them and come here to talk, and the little bird-daughter tells them things that only she can see. Francisca was laughing, doubtful. But what about ghosts, aren't you afraid of them? Or of the skeletons that come up from underground and wear dirty rags and walk like this, uuuuh, uuuuh! They're underground, stuck right here, aren't you afraid of dead people? Lígia laughed loudly, that's dumb, it's not true—and looked at me to confirm. The oldest meaning of *educate* is to pull up, to draw something out: a sword from its sheath (*gladium e vagina educere*), a child from the mother's womb (*educit obstetrix*). The transformation of her laugh upon realizing my deep sadness. But I'm right here, Lígia, I'll always be … my gaze tried to complete the thought, but she no longer saw me.

If it were possible. My story perceived as a thing, without words, voiceless, but apprehended whole, solid. She's going to ask: Where did you go to college? Why did you choose education? Which professors left an impression on you? Where do these concepts come from—the importance of prison? Of the resistance? What can I say about Lígia's expression when she saw her first burial? When her understanding finally linked the deceased to the corpse, memory to rot.

I retired out of cowardice. Some of my colleagues were calling for a revolt, ready to fight for their rights, fair compensation for services rendered, the dignity of intellectual labor. In my case it was cowardice. They were going to do exactly what they wanted: change the rules for retiring and shaft the emeritus faculty. The truth is that it all bored me, I didn't see the point of getting involved. But it's easy to be bored when your own retirement is already guaranteed. Thirty-five years at the university, fifteen at the high school. During high school, I worked in a bank, and during college I gave test prep lessons at the community center so that I could buy my own books and not be a burden at home. My father was calm and had friends. He worked for the Post Office and belonged to a labor union. On Saturday evenings he hosted a *choro* circle with his friends at our house. On Sundays we'd go out, walking or by bus, to see the city. My father liked the stairway at the Museu do Ipiranga, the tributary waters of the Amazon trapped in aquaria, rising and dividing with the curves of the grand banister. We rarely went into the museum proper. My mother liked to go in and see the costume collection, but we'd wait for her outside, wandering between the houses of rich Arabs and through the well-kept parks. In '70, after I came home, he had a stroke, his hands went rigid and he could no longer play the flute. His mouth, severely twisted at the start, slowly returned to something like its former shape, but it never went back to normal. Forced to take disability, he retired, and died a few months later.

Armando played ukelele. Armando drew. Armando had girlfriends. Many. He had everything. He liked my family. He was loved. Armando was loved everywhere. He never managed to be invited into my father's *choro* circle, only because it wasn't possible, but my father still enjoyed himself with Armando on the nights he stayed late after studying. I hear my father's flute, his sharp trills, joyful—a spritely, fluid story. The complete opposite of his deep, clipped speech. I remember the sound of Armando's ukulele and his concentrated expression loosening into a malicious and waggish smile whenever he managed to accompany my father. My father would say, the boy's got something, maybe he'll really be able to play one day.

The flute never left its black case during the week. When he was young he'd played for a professional group. No such thing exists in Brazil, Joana, enough boasting, a professional is someone who lives from his work—do you know anyone who makes a decent living that way? No? Well then you'd better choose your words carefully before talking and in this case there's nothing to talk about anyway. You were in love, so you misremember things. They played at parties, public events, my mother would tell us when our father wasn't around. I imagine he'd had artistic and intellectual ambitions he kept under strict control, the way an alcoholic negotiates drinking. The Saturday *choro* circle attested to the fact that he wasn't a real alcoholic, he was capable of indulging moderately for social enjoyment, not out of desperate necessity. He'd studied a lot in his youth: he was a poor boy from the country who managed to get a job in the postal service so that he could continue his training. He devoted himself to music with the constancy of someone building his future, someone who isn't in a hurry, because he knows it's inevitable, who doesn't get distracted, because without that breath he pulled through puckered lips, he lacks oxygen, gets giddy, and doesn't know how to live. With the joy of an extremely timid person who finally steals a kiss from his crush after months of longing, that kiss—warmth spreading through the entire body, and the other, her smooth skin—that supreme delight, no need to say it. My father was happy, Dona Joana told us, and always calm, he walked tall among his many friends, he played, and when he laughed his eyes shone.

What happened? *Our mother, tell us quickly, our father, here he comes now.* This is literally from José's book, whether quoted or taken from memory—it doesn't matter. It invades my thoughts and takes me where I don't want to go. But I let it pass, let it speak. I don't want this version: this childhood, this father, this mother. May it sing instead, something prohibited in my father's *choro* circle.

"What happened, my son, is that one day the time came when dying wouldn't do any good, a time when life became order. Just life, without mystification." And then there was

José's father, "the man behind the mustache" (something he never wore), "serious, simple, and strong, who almost never speaks" (Drummond by José).

I don't know if my father was the strong type. Was he, like all of us among the living, simple? Who is simple? All right, that's enough José, please. I don't mean to get worked up: I like the character José created, his father—or, I should say, I don't like him so much as find the construction of this family tree intriguing. It's almost charming to see the way we've been sketched by my brother's gaze. We are links in the evolutionary chain that leads to him, *homo sapiens, homo sexualis*. Thus my father is transformed into a man from Itabira, *this pride, this hanging head with fatigued retinas*. His eyes were afflicted, glazed, distracted, closed. I wouldn't use *fatigued*, José. Our father's eyes were gray.

José mixes the expressions of different poets and writers in his work, he doesn't credit them or use italics. He says that the written word is like money: it's not the property of whoever coined it, but belongs to the person using it. He always was a little thief, it's true, always had an alibi at the ready. It was his fault I once got my nose broken and gave a boy on our street a black eye. Agnello, the other boy, had special marbles that were different than everyone else's—who knows where he got them. He accused José of having stolen some. José denied it, said it was a lie, that Agnello had cheated in the last game and was creating a distraction with this lie. He tackled José and I ended up in the middle of it. José knew I would get involved—he only stood up to Agnello because I was there. I told him to give back the marbles. José, red with hatred, said he didn't have them. He turned his pockets inside out to show that all he had were regular marbles. I knew something was up. I recognized the attitude of indignation and injustice that appeared each time he came home from school with low grades: he was always prepared with a tall tale of persecution or the like. I still doubted him, though he made his denials boldly, eyes glistening with hatred for my lack of solidarity. José's fists were clenched but his body betrayed that he was afraid and ready to flee. I was ashamed of him, of his head cowering between his shoulders, of the way he attacked from a defensive posture. Agnello did something he shouldn't have: he reached out to give José a light slap on the face and teased him, you're gonna cry, aren't you, little baby? I punched him in the face before I could think and since I didn't know how to fight, I ended up with a broken nose. Because although we played ball together, although we earned pocket money together by keeping an eye on people's cars while they went market down the street, although we played war, hide-and-seek, and everything else, we also fought. Fighting was a ritual among us: a time was set, people watched, we had rival clans—but I wasn't part of this ritual, and because I was always strong, no one ever messed with me. I think that was the first time I'd really needed to fight. Days later, with an itchy bandage on my nose, I saw Agnello's marbles in the room I shared with José, and laughed. I couldn't even get mad at José, only laugh at my own stupidity. When I told him that he really was a big son of a bitch, José countered that Agnello was a bully who thought he could cheat anybody smaller, and that he deserved to be taught a lesson. And what did I have to do with it, José? You're the older brother.

I went to the cemetery on Eliana's birthday to see the makeshift grave we'd made her. This was a few days ago. After Lígia witnessed her first coffin descend into the earth—the old ropes rubbing the varnish, the undertakers' dirty clothes, the way they hopped over the open grave, the tombstone, the cement spread with care, and the earth covering it up again, hiding everything, pretending that it's all just dirt—she felt cheated by our tribute. In the universe of childish superstitions, where concrete tombs grew out of the dirt, she feared some kind of divine retribution. She didn't want to go for strolls in the cemeteries anymore, and she began to doubt my explanations of even the most trivial things—after death our bodies are eaten by insects and worms, we're born from our mothers' bellies, every ring on the rattlesnake's rattler represents a year of life—and, against my wishes, she asked her grandmother if she could be baptized, she learned to pray, and crossed herself devoutly whenever she passed a cemetery or a church.

She was baptized at six along with her cousin Renato, the son Armando had with Luiza, born six months after his father's death. When Luiza returned to Brazil from France, he was already five years old. Our comrade had returned to get back in touch with her roots. She baptized her son and paraded with a samba school at Carnaval—rituals that slaked her thirst. Luiza was one of Armando's many simultaneous girlfriends. She wanted to make a family for herself and her son. With her quiet goodwill, my mother accepted these additions to our Sunday dinners. The boy was her granddaughter's cousin, after all. But obviously things didn't stop there: Renato went to a French day school—his mother's thirsting roots were not so parched as to compromise her little one's brilliant future—but on several afternoons each week Luiza couldn't pick him up from school. She had an arrangement with a taxi driver who picked him up and took him to Dona Joana's house, where he spent the rest of the day, took his bath, and ate his dinner. Often it wasn't until he was already asleep that she came to fetch him, smiling but exhausted, worn down by the various jobs she worked so she could pay for his schooling and build a life that seemed strange to me. Her ambitions, her certainty about where she wanted to end up and what she needed to do to get there—all of it was strange to me. The cold revolutionary determination was still there, but it was now put to work making money and advancing her career: her drive seemed to bloom from those those cadavers, a violent and powerful manure.

We are all one with the universe. *Living by death and dying by life* (Heraclitus of Ephesus). We rejuvenate ourselves seventy times per minute and this is what exhausts us. Our cells reconstitute the molecules of our bodies (ourselves), which die second by second, our cells degrade and ceaselessly transform. "We" never are: we are only our bodies, the same as a second ago, *dying of so much rejuvenation. If it weren't for death we wouldn't live* (Edgar Morin). Every error builds a safe step on which I ascend and ascend and ascend—but where? A sound like glug, glug, glug, like the people in Lígia's cartoons. I'd like to find a way of speaking about the necessity of cadavers and killings in our intellectual and creative lives, for that pretty girl of Teresa's. But any word that gets at death is dangerously attractive to young minds. It's frighting to be in young hands, though inevitable. I completely understand Nelson Rodrigues's advice to youth: *grow old, my sons, grow old as fast as you can.* But, like an old asthmatic who refuses to give up his cigarettes, I am incapable of disbelieving in the improbable things they bring me.

During the week the flute never left its black case until my father met Armando. The prohibitions on the black case and its music were broken by the ignorance that any such taboo existed. I remember the shock in José's eyes, reflecting my own, that afternoon when my father came in and found us in the living room: I was reading, José was doing his homework, and Armando was tinkering with his ukelele. Armando, with his back to the door, hadn't noticed him enter. Instead of the usual succinct hello on his way to the kitchen, he signaled for us not to let on to Armando that he'd come in. With a bemused smile, he crossed his arms, stood and listened for a while, and then tiptoed to the credenza underneath the stairs, took his flute from the case and began to accompany Armando. Startled, my classmate paused for a second, but then, perceiving the challenge, he began to follow my father's rhythm, slow at first but soon reaching such a crescendo that Armando cried out, I can't keep up! I can't keep up, my fingers are burning! He tossed the ukelele onto the sofa and they both doubled over laughing. José and I looked on, stupefied.

I keep reading to find out how José will describe this scene. Maybe because he has such a lively imagination, his memory is better than mine. I don't remember my parents ever having said anything about not opening the black case or even once asking our father to play for us. We just knew the topic was off-limits, just like the black case. He only practiced after lunch on Saturdays, in the hour or two before his friends arrived for the *choro* circle. We'd be around, speaking softly or reading, my mother sewing something for us or doing the dishes from lunch. But we understood that he wasn't playing for us. It was like a silent meditation that we weren't to interrupt, someplace we shouldn't trespass. It's possible no one had ever said anything about it, but we just knew. I knew and I imagine José did, too, because we never asked him to play, even though for various reasons (these I remember well), we'd wanted him to. The isolation he maintained made for a kind of daydream. In those hours, I pretended to read while lying on the checkered wood floor, restraining the movement of my head and feet so that he wouldn't be able to tell I was enjoying myself as I kept time with the music. Somehow I knew that he wouldn't like it and was afraid he'd then stop playing when we were nearby.

Oblivious to all this, Armando opened our father's black case and music poured out. Music for Armando, music with Armando—a cheery complicity between master and disciple that I'd never known, and which never expanded to include me, never spread throughout the house or spilled over into other rooms, or any of our father's subsequent habits. Joaquim Ferreira's timidity, and his music, were translated for his children by Dona Joana, in all their depth and sensibility. She cultivated in us the fear of an awesome and powerful being, of the furies we should beware, lest we provoke them. Armando's presence, which already had made my childishness so apparent, had now transformed my father into a complex person.

If there were any doubts about Renato being Armando's son—and I entertained some, although they had more to do with things Luiza let slip than anything else—they vanished when the boy got to be eleven or twelve years old, the age when I met his father. Lígia began to look at him differently, and the little boy's politeness began to irritate me. In Renato I discovered what had aggravated me about his father and about things from that period I didn't know how to name. Seduction as survival strategy.

After a few months, Armando got tired of the ukelele. It was like him to get bored by passions. But what he'd opened in Joaquim Ferreira, that black box, wasn't as fickle: our father didn't understand that Armando's enthusiasm for music was merely a boyish caprice. The condescension of my friend—awkwardly thanking the flautist, who then laughed in that strange way, being out of the habit of laughter—my friend, who egged my father on with his ever more nimble but fickle ukelele: he began to pain me.

As adolescents we stick to our companions. Everything pulls us out of the house and we return full of power to a space that seems miserly and meager. As cells multiply, we catch the scent of things we don't understand but nevertheless desire. Eliana acquired a scent that drove me wild. I couldn't understand it or acknowledge it. She'd come and go and didn't seem to perceive her own scent: that was what got me. I adored the way her laughter began as hesitation and then opened, wide and wet. Her teeth are always so white in my memory. Wet little things shaped like I don't know what—something delicious and untouchable. Others began to imitate her delayed laughter. She would blush and her skin, that color, is what remains most alive to me. Golden and smooth. The sunset caught in the reflection of a brass urn. Shining and nameless, that pink filling her cheeks and spreading across her radiant face. When I finally managed to touch that skin, I trembled. We tend to think of adolescents as foolish, but today I realize how much courage it took for me to touch her face. If something were to enchant me today with such intensity, I doubt I could muster the courage that I had then. I trembled: I wanted to go slowly, feel the soft hair that covered her skin, follow the route I'd mentally traced so many times, it was happening, she closed her eyes, half opened her lips, bringing me at last those precious shards of light—it was like that.

I found the letters, my reports. They're fine documents, nothing as serious as I remembered in terms of form, and rather pertinent in their content. Something wasn't working well in the engine of education. Humanitarian messianism, revolutionary catechism, and utilitarian pragmatism had all evaporated, and as the teachers crashed and burned, the blame was laid on the students. Parents charged us with the discipline they'd never imposed, students demanded respect they never offered, the teachers asked for meaning they couldn't find themselves. Everyone expected the schools to give them whatever they couldn't create in their own lives. With a tsunami's sterile violence, this dissatisfaction invaded the schools. The principals waged their battles without knowing what war they were fighting. Why educate? To create free men, revolutionaries, critics, useful citizens. Every decade had its objective. And now? There's no escape from complexity. The complexity of the world, of the country, of the city, of the neighborhood, of the family, of every subject, especially of the human experience; the complexity of childhood, of adolescence, of maturity, of old age and death. The sad sack man who has a brother, a father's brother, the mother's brother, son, envy, brother-in-law, he has to take a bath, shave, attend the meetings, sweep the breadcrumbs, he's jealous, he has money, lacks money, time, anger, boredom.

Eliana was natually timid. She was even quieter when she was around Armando, a little bit too attentive. She'd say that she was just paying attention, that she was interested in her brother's ideas, and always ready to bring him a drink and his special, toasted nuts. Armando's famous dishes changed from house to house. An eclectic palate, perhaps. Or like Don Juan, a gift for extracting the best from every cook. Anyway, Eliana didn't like to cook and in our house he drank beer and ate the large cashews that Eliana had learned how to toast whenever he wanted them. With Dona Esther, Eliana was impatient. Yet with both her brother and her mother she became childish, played dumb.

To write the reports, I decided to speak with future teachers: students of history, geography, biology, chemistry, mathematics, physics, Portuguese—kids just twenty or twenty-one years old, who'd spent the whole year going to classes in elementary schools and high schools as part of their training. I stopped talking and tried to listen to the teachers in charge of the professional development courses, the ones on the front lines of the despair and boredom the educators were suffering. What did these people see and hear? I interviewed some principals and teachers. I frequented classrooms and hallways, reviewed library collections, surveyed order and cleanliness, visited computer labs. I went to teachers' meetings. I spoke with parents and students, with administrators, coordinators, pedagogues, heads and subheads of various bureaus in the Department of Education, and I got the impression—just like that girl of Teresa's—that I was more in search of questions than answers.

After the change in government, two years ago, they wanted me in the Department of Education. I immediately declined, then wondered why. Lígia got mad, but she has no idea of the hell of politics, of how little can be accomplished from within, and anyway it wasn't right for me, more a proposition than an invitation, and the Department was still just an ugly dogfight. Lígia reminds me a lot of Eliana—this obligation to serve, that proud selflessness that often becomes tiresome—the student who always ends up doing the work for the whole group and doesn't even get mad at them for using her. Lígia's irritation with me didn't have anything to do with ambition or power: she just thought I couldn't spend my whole life saying that everything was wrong in our education system and then let go the moment I'd been handed the reins. But I've been part of many different governments, I've thrashed and snapped plenty of reins, and I know I can do much more from outside. Lígia said that things are different now that we're in power. But, my dear, who is this "we"?

Power, in my nightmares, resembles a great mass of energy, a black hole, turning and evolving through random movements corresponding to the strength of agitation made by all the groups it sucks into its vortex, deliriously smashing and pulverizing away like an abortion curette. I hear *the uterine scream when the curette makes contact with living tissue, the crack of little skeletons when they break into pieces* (Pedro Nava). My head pounding, I wake up sweaty, still resisting that sucking force carrying away my body. Like my father, I am not a good negotiator. I was never good with triangles, to say nothing of more complex polygons. I don't think men of action—and of meetings—are any braver or more ignorant than me, only different. Lígia says I'm afraid. Eliana said so, too, when I preferred to stay in the high schools rather than accept a university position, something I only did much later. In fact, I am afraid of becoming enthusiastic and destroying everything around me. Starting with myself.

I suggested someone else for the job: Otávio, one of my advisees years ago. He was involved in the Workers' Party and knew how to fight. He was appointed, provided that I promise to advise him. These things never work out, but I accepted the task of writing up a diagnostic of the middle schools in the municipal system. Over the course of a year, I sent my reports in the form of letters. Over the course of a year, as his ambition lost its shine, he became irritated with my letters and asked me to use formal documentation. He no longer wished to have a dialog, only an evaluation he could use as a weapon. I assented, I did what everyone else does: I diagnosed chaos. Otávio was furious.

I don't know who was right. I understand Otávio's logic,

the lines of thought array themselves like trenches, and we become permanent warriors. According to such logic, we already know everything beforehand and we state what we know (or not) according to combat conditions. In letters between two named interlocutors, *you* and *me*, I described meetings, transcribed subjective impressions and opinions overheard, and I discussed the origins of certain ideas that had taken shape over the course of my diagnostic research. What I had in mind was a dialog. It wasn't a question, as Otávio thought, of a lack of engagement, of a laziness for formalizing possible strategies. I really had doubts and I thought it would be healthy for him to entertain them, too. I didn't intend to construct some kind of weaponry, but to understand what type of war we were in, and to resolve the small concerns that would guide us in addressing the larger ones.

We suffer from new diseases: it isn't merely that the symptoms shift and deceive. How to diagnose things still nameless? I really distrust this excessive formalization, disconnecting us from the world. Government bodies suffer from an absence of reality, not from a surfeit of it, as many first believe when they arrive. They think they're prevented from thinking by the crushing demands, the excess of the world. But it's the opposite. The university has ended up the same way, losing contact: it still attempts to encompass some universal "everything" but we always manage to remain far from humankind, from life. My letters had the objective of bringing Otávio *into* the schools, situating his ear in the meeting rooms, at recess, in the conversations of the mothers who stood waiting for their children. Clearly, that's my way of apprehending the world, suggesting small strategies for specific cases. I'd draw generalizations from each little universe—personal stories, just a few, the ones with rich material. It's possible to discover interesting mechanisms through interviews. I'd have liked Otávio to respond to the letters with the intelligence I saw in him, and with the point of view of someone looking down from above, commanding a powerful bureaucracy with good intentions. I knew beforehand that my ideas would never have much of an effect on this vast machine, but I believed that contact with the repetitive small reality of a classroom might have some power. Focused contact: every case—each deposition—would begin a specific discussion about the necessity of revising the total ideological machinery that sustains the detached attitudes of teacher, principal, administrators. But our desire to mix our personal and social miseries diminishes with every day that goes by.

I didn't work out. Otávio would say that we'd had all the time in the world for questions—now was the time to act. But interrogation, doubt, and listening are actions. At that time, his main focus was defeating corporatism (which he viewed as having atrophied the joints in the bodies and minds of our profession) and transforming the school into an inclusive space.

My ill-tempered outbursts have become more frequent. I should carefully and rationally reconsider the things that irritate me. *Inclusion* is one of them. I become possessed when I see that word, transformed into a detestable person. Because if my bad moods are triggered by an impotence for doing good, it's a feeling compounded by the question of what should be done about what's good. Rage is never holy, only human—our last recourse for affirming that we are ourselves and not another—and rarely is it creative.

Maybe being rich is good for rational thinking, unlike what Dona Joana always thought. Liberated, not under so much pressure, free to stop and look around. Rich, idle, retired. It's a lie: nobody stops.

Three years ago, I was wandering the halls, observing the sequence of rooms, the teachers and students. A lightbulb in one of the classrooms exploded. It spat shards of glass over everything: the teacher panicked, students screamed, and when everyone finally calmed down the classic question came: Who did it? Murmurs, whispers, lowered heads, giggles. The outraged teacher insisted: Who was it? They pointed at Benício. Was it you? It was him. Why did you do it? He was silent. Go to the principal's office and wait for him. Benício got up slowly, head hanging. I appeared in the doorway. I'll save you some time, let's walk together. Back in my office, with the door closed, I asked: Was it you who broke the lightbulb? He nodded. You sure about that? He shot me an angry yes, without looking me in the eye. He was already a big boy, in that phase where they're all arms and legs, seated awkwardly in the chair, not fitting anywhere. He wanted to be reprimanded, get suspended, and be done with it. I said: It wasn't you. I saw: it was Manuel. Why are you lying? His eyes popped, he stared at me with fear and rage. I maintained my gaze, awaiting his response. Benício dropped his eyes and went mute.

It was a long conversation. Only after promising that I wouldn't go after his classmate, that I would still punish only him, Benício, that this would be our secret—little by little there tumbled out sentences in which I could discern the long and determined path he'd traversed to become the clown among the dunces. He'd never been accepted in any group, and adolescence had only worsened the situation, his affliction growing along with his arms, legs, nose, hair, prick, and pimples, all out of order and proportion. The role of class clown settled into place, the clown among the hooligan set. In eighth grade, the boys were already scoring with the girls, flirting and fighting and all that. During gym class they made him play goalie as a form of humiliation, and any trouble with the teachers always ended up on him, which is to say that he remained an object of scorn but was now a part of a group. He had penetrated the group, inserting himself, and he wasn't inclined to relinquish this conquest. I tried to make him see what his classmates were doing to him, that there was no advantage to belonging to a group like that, but he seemed highly conscious of what he was, a nobody, and he liked his buddies, admired them and felt accepted by them exactly as he was: a nobody. Anyone who tried to convince him that he had the ability to be much more, not a nobody, and even more of a somebody than his classmates, would be classified as an enemy.

I spoke with his teachers. Benício was considered a mediocre student, timid and without much interest in any of his subjects. Though his social studies teacher found him to be intelligent, saying that he learned new concepts quickly and had a good memory, Benício's insecurity was so great that he made mistakes on his tests and never managed to finish one. He did better on individual projects and with homework. The math teacher complained about his messy work. He'd pile the sums up on top of each other, scratching out numbers instead of erasing them, and as a consequence, his work was so sloppy that, naturally, he got the wrong answers. It seemed like he understood the logic of math, but it was difficult to evaluate him due to his careless work and reticence in class. His Portuguese teacher thought that Benício had some kind of neurological problem, given that his development was so uneven. He didn't make common spelling mistakes, and carefully incorporated new words into his compositions. He used correct subject–verb agreement, something that most of the students couldn't do. But on the other hand, he switched his Ds and Ts, his Fs and Vs, his Ps and Bs. And his essays were full of non sequiturs. One sentence never linked to the next, he'd completely change the subject, begin by proposing one idea and conclude with its refutation. He gen-

erally only wrote the absolute minimum required, stories full of clichés, in tiny, ugly, blotched handwriting. His teachers all agreed that he was a student who did his work without the least concern about turning in complete garbage for the entire past year.

They realized that they became more irritated with him than with the ones who probably provoked this mess—Benício didn't have the smarts to manage his own disorder and could never tell when the time for fun and games had passed. He was never the instigator, but, entering into the ruckus, he got rambunctious and never knew when to quit. Then, after being possessed by some kind of borrowed agitation he couldn't control, he'd realize that everyone else had gotten quiet. After being scolded he'd get embarrassed and turn red, which provoked the laughter of his classmates. And later, when the lesson got started again, he'd smile victoriously to his buddies, but they paid him no attention. His phys ed teacher, who'd known the boy for a while, since fifth grade, said he'd always been maladjusted, but that he used to make an effort to do well. Benício was incapable of reacting to their taunts, he'd get offended when they tormented him, but he'd still make an effort to succeed. Lately he'd gotten caught up copying his classmates' pranks and couldn't concentrate on the game. He'd already gotten a few demerits and the gym teacher had benched him. There was consensus that the boy had never had much of a future. Benício was bullheaded, he'd earned his reputation but not a single ally. Everyone had already given up on him, and now they rejected him. It would be difficult to wrench his conquest away.

I called his parents and tried talking to them. The father's response: "Yeah, I know, he's a jackass. At home it's the same thing. I say to him, what are you, some kind of moron? But it doesn't make any difference, kids don't listen to their parents, and he never tells me anything." Benício's victory at home was assured.

I asked his teachers to help reinforce the boy's positive attitudes, to call attention to him publicly, and single him out for his cooperation. Whenever he became difficult he was to be ignored. I asked his parents to do the same. They weren't very convinced but agreed to send him to a psychologist. I used all my influence to get one, and even then it was necessary to give him money for the bus. We arranged it all. It was a second-rate psychologist, because I didn't foresee any great difficulties with the case. At first, Benício was furious about our "intervention." He stopped doing his homework and became even more rowdy in class—he started being the instigator. This was an advancement: he was finally at the head of something. This pulling of the rug destabilized him, confirming how important it was for him to be the class clown. He started to fight with his teachers and behave violently. He knew he needed to act this way to save face but he didn't have any control over his actions. We changed tack. He began to be punished for acts that were legitimately his, and his grades suffered. His conversations with the psychologist were no longer about being the clown, but about being violent. This difference was important to Benício. In student-teacher meetings his teachers continued to reinforce his positive traits and returned his homework with personalized remarks.

Failing grades were important to his recovery. Benício went from being a mediocre student to running the risk of having to repeat the year. We began to understand that no matter how strong his determination to belong to that group, he'd left an escape hatch open in the event of emergencies. No matter how much contempt he showed for his assignments, passing would prove that he was not a complete moron, that his father was wrong, that some day he'd be able to turn things around. There's a perverse mechanism in the schools with regard to this type of student, the ones the teachers have already written off. If they didn't put up a fight, if they were agreeable, they'd usually get *the minimum passing grade. It was useful to have a case like Benício's to observe and discuss. It demonstrated the damage that a lack of honest evaluation can have on a young person.*

After a long struggle, Benício found a balance between what the school, his parents, and his friends all expected of him. By forcing this triangulation, we threw Benício into the void. He lost his name, his lodestar, and had to start over. The rowdy ones settled down, as often occurs at this age, and new students entered the school. Classes were shuffled, some kids changed schools, and in the end, each one has his own story. We don't always get to see them so clearly, dissecting them, photographing precise moments, as we were able to do in Benício's case. I think he's doing well now—he'll be accepted on the team as long as he's a good goalie, and accepted by his teachers as long as he's doing his homework. He'll be accepted in life as long as it lasts. He's the goalie on our handball team and talks about going on to college. He never got over his shyness, but he can look you in the eye now. He avoids me as best he can and at recess he brags about his biggest stunt, the time he made a light bulb explode, giving the teacher a nervous breakdown, and getting chewed out by the principal.

Me—*evaluation notes*, circa 1980

Perhaps I hesitated in sending these letters because it was a form of betraying Otávio. Perhaps because sending them was a way of exchanging interlocutors, and even genres. It's fiction, what the girl writes: just like José. Maybe that's the only way so-called humanity can face itself, allowing us to talk about what really matters. I don't know how to tell a story or write one, either. A story, that thing closed up in itself. But I can collaborate in my own way. Yes, the letters will be good material for her, and maybe they'll allow me to escape being interviewed. They're exactly what she needs, the daily grind at the school, et cetera and so on. I don't want to talk about what I've already forgotten.

I want, I don't want, I want, I want. That's how José writes. Everything is in the wanting. In his book we're three brothers. Twins called Amado and G, in addition to the one who narrates. The mother and father are our mother and father, likewise without names. Amado and the mother are solar figures who protect the narrator from the *black light of a cruel destiny* thrown off by G and the father. Black light is what *illuminates the bloodless theater* where the narrator acts out *the role of a fool in love*. And oh! From the first pages he suggests that good will prevail and that *love will be made eternal once more*. I realize it's better than saying eternal for as long as it lasts—it's perfect, like everything else Nelson Cavaquinho sings about. But it's a tic that bothers me about José: leaving a contradiction in terms hanging there, with an air of supreme poetic intelligence. And tossing off, without attribution, a verse from Vinícius de Moraes, a verse that tugs on the entire universe of a single author—if only for the initiated. José however claims that even the uninitiated can appropriate and make use of a single verse: it's the way an expression becomes common speech, the way any new slang enters the language.

The mother is very well done. Maybe because he'd gone without seeing her for so long, José was able to capture her younger self, with a clarity that I'd either lost or never had. Reading her, I laugh to myself at my young mother. Her daydreams and coquetry. Always wearing a cameo necklace draped over dresses she'd sewn herself. José remembers the patterns and styles: he fills entire pages with the delicate elegance of a woman who deftly played the bad hand life had dealt her, warding off misery with a needle, fabric, and dreams. Always motherly light and fatherly shadow. The father José depicts is powerful enough to subdue and restrict the mother's light. Her sewing, her proud posture, the melodies she distractedly hummed, broken by fugues and feints, are her ways of evading oppression and staying sane. There is no harmony. The father and the fag are almost nothing in themselves, only lifeless puppets of a cruel destiny that renders the theater bloodless. There is no blame, they're just part of the world, or its impossibility. Above all, they're opaque.

I become annoyed by the simplicity of the story of José and his brothers. When simplified, the terms become the exact opposite of my own, and in those terms, my own, the story is banal. But see for yourselves:

> *The first sound, still blended with my dreams, the sound that accompanies my rest upon the earth—I'm not yet lying in bed, at home, between four walls, but with a blanket, pillow, and music that returns to me my body: it's the pitter-patter on the stairs announcing my mother's approach. I half open my eyes as her dress brushes against the footboard on the bed, leaving behind a soft morning scent and sending the dust dancing through the light streaming in between the blinds. G. is already in the shower and mother's dress, her thighs and her back, undulate beside Amado. Our room is snug, and her body makes tight, gentle turns until she's seated on my brother's bed, leaning over to tousle Amado's hair and whispering, wake up, it's time for school. Amado prolongs the caress by rolling over and moaning, not yet, just a little longer, but she's back on her feet. And then she turns to me, her face appearing over me. The blinds are tall and she is short, and the morning light creates a halo around her hair, gathered back in a bun. Her head floats in the air, her bright eyes and parsimonious smile intensify this cloud which does not darken, but attracts, absorbs, and clashes with the solid mass that comes to hug me, raising me up from bed with earthy*

warmth. The morning ritual is broken off, hurried, or modified if G. comes in before it's over: dressed, clean, silent, and smelling of coconut soap. He puts his folded pajamas away in the drawer, straightens up the bed without bending to kiss his mother. He says only "morning" to her "good morning." G.'s morning mills this mixture of earth and sky with what remains of nighttime and slumber, and the day asserts itself with the slam of a door downstairs and the smell of the bread that my father eats behind his morning newspaper—mask. I never saw G.'s body, he got dressed in the bathroom and slept in his pajamas. Amado's body, at breakfast, still smelled of sleep—I think he only ever wet his hair at the sink to smooth his cowlicks and pretended to have showered. Amado's body is where my perception of my own begins. G.'s body was its limit. I came from my mother's body and would end up in my father's.

Such were mornings in our house: talking and listening, everything moving and changing. I began speaking late, and unlike my brothers, I had difficulty learning to write. Our household wasn't one of many words, but it communicated in other ways. The stairway announced who came and went, the smell of each client stated what kind of work our mother was brought, and at night the way the door opened to admit our father determined what time we'd go to our rooms. In the dark our house grew and was taken over by its true owners: the floor, the walls, the pots and pans, the armchair, the door, the roof, the cracks. They don't do anything, they're neither good nor bad, they merely expand, occupy more space, like a foot that emerges from a split shoe. They make themselves comfortable and discuss their own affairs. The sleeping bodies were likewise among the owners of the house, because the bodies weren't people. They weren't mother, father, son, and brother: only bodies.

The morning dust brought us back and the house returned to a shape our eyes recognized, but only in the places we passed through. Except for me: I was small and still didn't have the power to intimidate those things, to make them cease exuding their own personalities, not even with the help of the morning light. Mother, father, and Amado had this natural ability to transform a door into a door, the floor into the floor. But not G. He was turned too far inward to notice anything different, and had no concerns about whether things around him behaved one way or another. He's the only one to whom the stairway never sang when he went up and down.

José—*unpublished manuscript*

The father had the smell of bread, Amado that of sleep. And the mother, she smelled warm and soft. Only G. smelled of coconut soap, something that strips away all other scents, a smell of a thing and not the smell of a person. G. doesn't have a scent, a sound, or a body. He nearly lacks a name. Only an initial. Is that what I was? I worry about what remains, what's left behind. About what Marta will remember of her grandfather. I usually don't worry about things I can't control—my image, for one. It's an old agreement I made with myself, one that's now begun to waver. That girl of Teresa's, the argument with Otávio, my retirement, being the grandfather of a girl who is another man's child. But what am I saying? Look here, Armando would say, look here, whenever he began a lie.

The girl called, saying that she hadn't received the letter–reports I promised, maybe some kind of problem with her email. No, I still haven't sent them, I lost your address, I lied. Her name was Cecília. On the telephone she sounds older, her voice lower, slightly hoarse. She was also more formal. Losing her address was a terrible excuse. It demonstrates a disinterest that I'd like to have but don't. Maybe this was the reason she drew back, and why Teresa remained absent between us. I tried to redeem myself. I said I'd send them today. And now I've just sent them—come what may. Anyway, it's just foolishness, only a girl and her novel. She's already spoken with others. I'll just be one of those clueless cultural subjects like the ones the anthropologists interview in their research—like those teachers and principals who maybe only told me what I wanted to hear. Illustrations, an actor from a decade I don't even remember, from a story I never chose.

To be honest I don't really remember what José was like when he was little. It's as though he hadn't existed. From elementary school I remember more. He was always glued to Armando, and that embarrassed me. I remember things from before that, too: holidays we spent in São Carlos, Grandma Ana's house, the way she taught him to read. It seemed to me that he knew how to read perfectly well, and was only too stubborn to do it on command. Back then I thought that stubbornness was an expression of will, a personal decision, the fruit of freedom. I had to force myself to work hard at my studies and I found it unfair that Grandma Ana would give more attention to the one who wasn't asking for anything, who wanted the world on his own time. After they figured out he was nearsighted, he was always losing his glasses. He'd find a way to break them, and with all the household money spoken for, it wasn't unusual to see him wearing glasses held together with surgical tape. A strange bird: maybe that was my feeling with regard to José.

With Jussara things were different. She was younger, just a child. We became close when we were older. We all liked her—except maybe for José. He comes and goes, and disappears for long periods of time. I said that maybe he didn't like Jussara because in my memory he was a being that disliked everything about its situation in the world. But I retain only a few scenes of my youth in which I can see that clearly. He's only two years younger, we went to school together, I know that we shared the same room and I remember quite well his spot at the table—but not much about him.

We likely choose our enemies the same way we choose friends. What I mean is that the enemies we select are a fundamental part of our formation: the counterexample is as essential as the example. Enemies can be as liberating as friends can be constraining. I hope I've been able to help José as his enemy-elect. Armando was my friend. We shouldn't be afraid when a student selects us as an enemy, and sometimes it's wise to be cautious when they offer friendship. It doesn't always go well. Evil is on the loose, it's in our hearts, and we aren't entirely adults at every moment—when we accept a challenge to combat, or pick a fight with a student, we're capable of hurting them more than we realize, interrupting their flow and sending them into an abyss from which they sometimes can't climb back out.

Even immobility is flux. Flowing amid what reconstitutes us daily. Here and now are never only here and now. We do not possesses the neurological ability for inertia (except those who've suffer trauma). The blind who regain their sight have enormous difficulties with things in movement. To a blind man, a teacup is its volume, and his estimation of its capacity doesn't change according to his position. Abyss. Immobility is stopped movement—everything flows, it's necessary to put up resistance in order not to be carried along with the flow—and resistance is a movement. Holding still and thinking without writing. Thinking almost without thinking: the abyss returns and draws me in. There are so many things we don't do in life. One boy needed glasses and only after six months could I get him an appointment. Six months at eight years old, an eternity for not knowing what you can't see, for thinking yourself stupid, inferior. I wasn't able to get Mauro's stepfather jailed. His mother promised the judge that she'd start giving the boy a bath, and take good care of him. The judge scowled, losing his composure. The mother said yes sir, and Mauro continued to be abused by his stepfather. With a child like that, it's impossible to reconstruct his ways of perceiving the world. He came to us already offering himself, slouching into others, brushing against them. He got his ears cuffed, waited out benders, was struck by slurs and stones. It's what he knew. , bend over, take it. He was a slight boy, and provoked his classmates' violence. He got too close to their desires. The nicer teachers, the ones with a softer touch, who took time out for each student—they were the ones who got it the worst. Later the bony yellow hand, scrawny but with a blind man's sense for the body's pathways, stumbled over nipples, earlobes: mouth smeared across mouth in the moment of embrace. They got scared, angrily threw him off, suddenly understanding the cruel nicknames: Little faggot, little fag. How could the boy be reached? Only Mauro knew.

The stricter teachers had a better chance. Posture, limits, concentration, silence, order. The law of the group. It didn't matter if one kid was shortsighted, the other dyslexic, or if the third had watched his father beat his mother the night before. In school everyone was equal and there was work to be done. The tough teachers helped him more than the sweet ones. The rules were clear and the prejudices all had names. Filthy, scrawny, black, lazy, weakling, wannabe, half-starved, dirty-minded, loser, faggot, idiot. A name is a model as well as a mirror: it's a place in the world. What can be named exists. It is fixed, precise. Perhaps this is why it reassures, whereas the condescension of the nice teachers only disavows. When they condescendingly deny the name they introduce the vague and terrifying model of nullity.

Me—*evaluation notes,* undated

Those of us who work in education are an emphatic, opinionated, and by nature optimistic class of workers: a noisy bunch, both men and women, since our voices are our instruments. It's a bit like being an actor, though always playing for the youngest audience. How can it be that we manage to change so little? I don't mean opinions, but the concept of education itself: the classrooms, the buildings, the schedules, the rows of desks, the various channels of control of the universities. I'm not talking about buying computers, putting TVs in the classrooms, holding lessons under a tree. The stakes of what we failed to change are much higher. Maybe the methods of evaluation are correct and the problem is all the repetition. We repeat the same material our whole lives. We flip the calendar to hide the evidence, that it's years of our own lives that we repeat, not merely the material. We ought to be preparing children for the world. We're a public space for socialization, knowledge, life: children come into contact here with an unfamiliar organization and develop new ways of relating to each other, their identities reflected in different forms, building new possibilities for subjectivity to carry into the world.

But if we think in silence, without speaking, out in the open with just a scarf and our ID, intact and insensible to our surroundings, closed off in our fusty interiors, then one day—and not one rainy day, because catching a cold doesn't strengthen the powers of reason—one fine day on which the sun only appears in the colors and shapes of things, without any shining, your hands, still stiff perhaps, rubbing together, or gesticulating, or cradling your chin, scratching your ear and your head in involuntary trajectories originating in your tangled thoughts as you wander through a São Paulo cemetery on a gray Wednesday in July—if we think in this way, we can inquire deep within ourselves about what exactly makes up the condition of this world, of this *life* that we've consigned to the schools. The obvious first question concerning the schools is this: are we the world or do we prepare for the world? That is, are we the world or its didactic simulation? And is family a part of this world or not?

Yes, we could limit the question to public and private. Maybe that way we'll correctly delimit our problem and return to that pair, the public and private, so precious to Brazilians—to their separation, intersection, and promiscuity—distinctions which are apparently the primordial basis for the construction of the civilized civilization that we are not.

My legs are still strong, but as the tangle of thoughts thickens I lighten my pace—my lungs can no longer keep up. The temptation comes to interrupt my stroll, to sit down on one of the benches, to lean my forehead into the palm of my hand and prop my elbow on my thigh—to use my arm to create that thigh-to-head circuit so propitious to thought. But my back hurts and I prefer to stand leaning against a grave, my right foot on the ground, leg locked, my left leg on the tomb, dividing my body's gravity in half. I recall one of Luis Fernando Verissimo's columns in the paper, about a man gazing into a fire and meditating on the gravity of human affairs, which will only be fully realized when we're fossils. *We too will imprison energy below the earth and we will be like coal, oil, and the decomposed remains of everything that ever lived, integrated into the explosive layer of the planet: what could be more grave? All organic material, from the jabuticaba tree to the potato, yearns for it, this subterranean respectability, this mineral dignity after the ephemeral frivolity of life. From dust to dust, but now after our time in the sun, as another category: combustibles.* I brood over this idea of death as becoming-flammable. Not exactly the fact in itself, but its association with our incessant hunger for minerals, and for returning to the great immobility we once were. To unite *fossil* with *explosion*. Death and dung are so common, and we appreciate the latter only for transforming organic matter once more: a tree bending over a grave, mineral as transition between human and plant. Fossils and combustion are less domestic images, more the slow and archaic aspects of a larger universe over which we have no control. Our time doesn't contain them, our view doesn't stretch. And suddenly a spark, a boom, sound and light, heat. Verissimo's column contains the thoughts of a man gazing at the fire. Had it been written in a wet month, it almost certainly would have mentioned the importance of air to this process. Air at the beginning and at the end.

A campfire, a bonfire: it only catches when the spaces for oxygen to pass between the logs are well calibrated. You have to think of which way the fire will collapse and which passages will close and open when it does. Maybe more sensation than thought, because not all the facts are at hand: which log is drier or more hollow than another, which way the wind will be blowing the hardest, where the fire will pull the hardest. So you have to weigh the kindling and the knots in the wood as you arrange the logs. And even, so adjustments are still necessary throughout the process, and extra attention paid if it's a wet month. And oxygen, at the end. Air, smell, heat, light, and sound.

Maybe we live in wet years, when you get down to it, and things are sticky, making calibration of the air difficult, and more necessary for turning oxygen to fire, for making our students sing, emit heat, and be consumed, emitting light. The sound that green wood makes: violent pops, squeals expelling sap, leaping flames, the solitary ember that scorches the carpet and later burns out. Fire can't resist: it dies, the charred logs cool. But this is just an image without much use, child's play of transforming one thing into another, a thing into words, words into history, history back into a thing. Classic images of education: student as the earth where we plant our seed, student as the seed we nourish and help to grow, student as the wild animal we tame, the clay we mold, the stone we sculpt, the bird we teach to fly. The wood that burns. It's not even a good metaphor. But it would be a big hit at a school assembly or in one of José's stories: talk and fiction, spaces for subjects and not ideas. The thought that creates generous paths on which others might tread, to attain new vistas, paving another few paces forward, or at least breaking new ground: this new thought is strange to the insensible and luminous subject that writes *I*, says *I*, thinks of itself as *I*, can discern things only from the perspectivse of the *I*. The idea of student-kindling exposes this sterile I.

The freedom of a story or a novel includes, by definition, the freedom of ambiguity and contradiction. The process of the human condition is what Cecília seeks in me and others. My ideas are worth no more than my feelings. She wants the sudden flash of character, fragments of a being in a world that she didn't know in its entirely, but whose echoes, both dead and surviving, form part of the structure he has inhabited, and where he continues to live. Long ago, novels, poetry, music, films, and plays changed the world, and education and work still contained this possibility, Cecília believes.

Here I must stop. The air reenters my lungs or, as Francisco Augusto says, exits. Shortness of breath is caused by a failure to expel air from the lungs: we hold on to used air—carbonic gas—leaving no room for oxygen to enter and run its course: the path to fossilization. When I think quickly, I walk quickly. Then something gets stuck, blocking the exchange. I observe this in students who are fast learners, the ones who easily apprehend new meanings, build connections, everything makes sense, connects to what was already there, generates new feelings, and then suddenly, they're halted. Some kind of resistance seems necessary: an estrangement, almost some kind of affront, the realization of the loss present in every gain.

But there's no way to argue against an idea in a novel. The idea can be fit into any worldview, assigned an origin and destination, a function in the action and composition of history. It can indicate certain new paths, useful to a thinker in the same way the violet winter sunset or a fire might forge a new link between our thought and its surroundings, which they nourish and provoke. But paths to an idea cannot be contradicted, shared, or even questioned: how can you doubt the sunrise, or argue with a begcourgar's rant, or with the stupor of a cuckolded friend? So many thoughts occur in these moments, pregnant with ideas. The line at the bank, the bakery counter, the birdsong, the priest beneath the stained glass.

When Renato was fourteen, Luiza got together with a diplomat and moved to China. She was always polyandrous, just as Armando had been polygamous. A flower with many stamens, sterile after Renato. The richness of a living being resides in its ability to spread its genetic inheritance. Luiza's was in accumulating, retaining. A uterus full of sperm, sucking at the tiny feet of the insects that landed there. Sometimes she went all the way to shacking up, buying a fridge, putting on the airs, clothing, and vocabulary of the wife of: lawyer, adman, economist, tycoon, financier, doctor, politician. Other times she only made room in her apartment for: students, writers, professors, artists, goldsmiths, fishermen. In state registries her civil status always remained "widow." Renato didn't want to go to China with his mother and stayed with Dona Joana. Lígia moved into her grandmother's room and Renato took the small one that had been Jussara's and was originally part of ours, José.

The house at first had four big bedrooms. When Jussara was born, they put the crib in our room. Her early morning cries were followed by soft, slippered footfalls and the sound of her suckling at our mother's breast. José will not remember this image: a sonorous and tactile sequence blended in with my dreams: the soft cry growing, the felt slippers on the wood floor, the weight of the two at the foot of the bed, *suck-suck*, I'd peer from half-opened eyes to see my mother and the baby, a single mass, the breast and the mouth, their gazes and giggles, the milk running from the corner of Jussara's mouth whenever mother stroked her cheek and made the baby laugh, her eyes sparkling some undetermined color. I'd pretend to be rolling over in my sleep and bring my feet against my mother's thighs, drawing warmth from the *suck-suck*, elongating the mass. I'd reawaken to the sound of my father knocking his toothbrush against the edge of the sink. I don't know exactly when they put up a wall to divide the room in two. In José's house, the one in his book, Jussara wasn't born: we are four men, plus our mother. And José was always the baby, sucking.

Anyway, Renato moved in with us for good. The agreement had already been reached when Dona Joana came to speak with me about it. Even after my father's death, domestic decisions weren't divided between us. And now that I think about it, our father was never one to make decisions, either. José sees the world through dominion and predominance, and maybe I understand things more like agreements, accommodations. A masculine laziness about the little things that make up life. More than indolence, really: it's irritation with the tedious polemics of small decisions, with having to leave my mark on everything, a tomcat pissing on the sofa legs.

To sign, that is the first meaning of *teach*: to leave a mark. More than a sign, a signal. But that's where things get complicated, where the conventional, social character of the sign is exposed, and I'm going too quickly, I'm out of breath again. Let's stick with sign, a sign that distinguishes a being, he has a sign, a sign given by the master, the one who instructs. Let's return to the first mark, not to Cain's—that would be the third, we'll get there. The first two, as I understand it, are the ones God made on Adam and Eve. The man who can only eat by the sweat of his labor and the woman who will give birth in pain. What did it mean, this mark? It distinguished them from those who had remained, the lambs of God who hadn't betrayed His trust. With Cain it was the same: he is marked for having betrayed. Jacob is marked by his father, and Joseph by his brothers. The sign of betrayal isn't the only kind, and it's not the one we have in mind when teaching our students. But it was the first—and it was the mark given to me, which is why I'd like to consider it.

Betrayal and tradition share the notion of transmission, the act of handing over. The old play on words—*traduttore, traditore*—takes its meaning not merely from the phonetic similarity between the two words, or the deeper meaning it gives to the act of translation. The similarity is plain and it's right there in the root of the words, both of which refer to the act of passing from one side to another. We know that this going-over is never innocent and that nothing that crosses over can ever come back unchanged. To distract is something else: close in origin, but different in meaning. At first it meant to pull apart different things; to break, to tear, to scratch, to destroy, to quarter, to sell in parcels, to distribute, to divide, to level, to compose, to be defamed. The mailman hands over the letter he transmits. But my father wasn't really a mailman: he worked at a desk, minding the flow of things and looking after union affairs.

I think about where Cecília's questions might take me. Back to a time when the schools harbored a detonating desire: that's more or less what she's looking for. We continue to detonate. Contact with knowledge is always something violent and transformative, no matter how bad we are as teachers. The students learn a new language, not only the specialized vocabularies of knowledge, in mathematics and writing, but another Portuguese: standard Portuguese. But whose standard is it? We abandon what we are, we betray our parents: that's what we learn. Grandma Ana's Jesus Christ would say that's what it means to grow up. And later maturation, aging, retirement, and a return to our parents. I adopted my father's habit of always walking with an umbrella, and ended up creating such an intimacy with my umbrella that I never forget it anywhere. This one has lasted almost a year.

I already miss my job, the schedule and routine. I've been concerning myself too much with this interview, which wouldn't be preoccupying me if I were still teaching classes and preparing for next semester. José's book hasn't helped either, not even as a counterpoint. Armando's always there, submerged in my thoughts, but he now returns in force. I think it might have been more tolerable—the weight of accusation, the mark of Cain—if it had been anybody else who'd gotten killed. I miss him: our conversations are now idiotic monologues, building fire with sticks, nursing a cold tomb. I lack a counterpoint, a brother in arms. The mark of damnation isn't as heavy as his absence. But I've had to carry both at the same time, as a single burden and I shouldered it, it's true,

I remained silent. I refused to respond to the never stated, always whispered accusation. It wasn't only disgust, although there was that, too, it's true: a violent physical nausea every time my responsibility for the crime phantasmagorically appeared in a gaze, in a slanted comment, in the absences of my supposed friends. I knew that I couldn't allow this chancre of rage to take over—I struggled against mistrust, against making enemies. But I was systematically defeated in those first years. Anybody might transform into an accuser: *Traitor*. I wouldn't rebel against it so much if the dead man were anyone else. Perhaps I'd be able to see the necessity for traitors from an anthropological point of view. I'd be able to sit down and discuss the matter, not to defend myself, because that will always be distasteful, but to try to show my friend how things look through my eyes, to remind him of who I am, to make him see. To see and not, believing what he's heard, just glare at me. To see—and ripping out the doubt with my bare hand, I'd say: listen, it's me and I'm here, the same old me. But no, any effort to deny a betrayal implies that it could have happened, and this is unthinkable to me: the iron brand that burns the steer's haunches. A physical pain, worse for being unexpected.

I was never a revolutionary, never took part in that enthusiasm. I never burned with the certainty of having a declared enemy. I was excited. We, mankind: we were going to change a lot more than the world. Each one of us had our own path, and we were all in it together—even if my path never took me down in the trenches the way so many others went involved in the various movements. Movements: we didn't always call it that. Those in the armed struggle said "organization," and then shut up. Today in the slums and the fields groups call themselves a movement. A curious expression, movement.

Everything that moves is divine—I think Newton had a problem with that: explaining the movement of the stars while maintaining their divine logic. I believe there's this idea that movement, more than any other manifestation, confirms the presence of the divine. Anyway the problem was this eccentricity with words: stopping before each one, taking it in my hands, massaging it, observing it from several angles, and only then, after it was deformed, allowing it to enter. As an eccentric, I felt ill suited to movements and organizations. Armando understood this, he accepted my way of participating where the movement unfolded in the community: by teaching, studying, raising a family. This isn't the whole truth. My classes were inflammatory, I participated in student politics, I was active at the student center, I traveled to student conferences. We had study groups, alliances with other student organizations, arguments in bars. And I wrote violent articles. I was the editor of the natural sciences student guild's newspaper. Brazil was coming into its own, and we were one of the first departments to move to the new campus: beautiful, big, and wild (when was this? '62? '63? Somewhere in there). We were in touch with the entire country.

Those were our feelings, and they certainly moved us: today we are in closer contact with the whole world. But my feeling is of no longer knowing my neighbor. I spoke of burning with the fire of having a declared enemy. They existed, our enemies, before 1964: the bourgeoisie, poverty, capitalism, ignorance, oppression. But I sincerely understood them, that was the only possible way for me: understanding that these antagonists dwelled within us and that the struggle to build a new life for the new world would be waged inside each one of us. My new man was beardless and nude. There was so much to learn, on every trip, in group meetings, in the bars, and even in the classrooms. There was biology, and the way each professor approached it, girls, and adulthood—but not my parents' adulthood. I taught college prep for the sciences and started working in a research lab. Before starting at the university, I worked in the bank and studied at night. Armando had a job, too, in a construction firm office. He organized the flow of materials, and I the flow of funds.

> *I worked in the bank and in the bank I was possessed. Banks are a trap, banks are a trap: I was certain, absolutely certain, convinced, that the money in the bank was mine. Why? Because they give you a certain authority which then gives you the feeling of power. My section was called "Accounts Payable." What did I do? I received instructions from agencies about which checks should be paid and about the limits on each account. I was seventeen, and to me this was thrilling: the power to say yes or no—it never occurred to me that what I was doing was just another dumb job. Fortunately I had a banker friend there, Mr. Gabriel. He was a cashier, and he'd say to me: Hey, watch out, in a banker's life the only thing that ever changes is the date on the stamp. My god, was it damning. Power wasn't in saying yes or no to a check, but to the person who presented it. Will I cash the check or won't I? It was a simulacrum of having money at my disposal, as though the money were mine. You go nuts like that.*
>
> Someone like me—*recent conversation*

At 7 Vaz Leme Street, in that house that still held three children, mother and father, plus Grandma Ana, who came to live with us, widowed and sick, and the Saturday *choro* sessions and the union guys and the nightly meetings, with my father shuffling papers, writing out minutes and declarations, my mother sewing, my grandmother helping José with his homework or putting Jussara to bed and telling her stories. And Ritinha, who helped my mother with the sewing and with chores around the house, folding laundry and sweeping up the day's loose ends, rushing off to her night-school course in typing. Number 7 Vaz Leme Street, full of such modest folk. A lineage without a single aristocrat or king. Cells, millions of them in a tiny dome under the microscope—working incessantly, dying, being born, transforming—always rounded shapes that absorb, expel, and return to their mobile, terrestrial lines, the crust of the entire planet consumed with such round, uninterrupted work. I left the bank and went into natural sciences: paying and not paying adapted to the prosaic work of cells, but the memory of power remained embedded, germinating a depression in the sheath of a memory until, little by little, that memory was assimilated and charged with the electric current of the movements.

For thirty years I've been getting my hair cut by Mr. Osvaldo, three blocks from number 7, Vaz Leme. Valfrido, the nephew of some relative of Osvaldo's wife, came on later. The two of them already old men, though Valfrido must be a few years younger me he already has the face of an old barber. Their relationship is old: Valfrido has always remained the young apprentice with a promising future if only he could settle down and learn to do things right. Maybe for this reason, now that he's in his fifties, I hunch over and with the characteristic grimace of life's commentators (taxi drivers, shoe shiners, bakery cashiers, newsstand men), those for whom life passes by in pieces each day (the elevator operators, too)—I make a face that, when you think about it, isn't really a grimace, and yet it's more than just a way of talking, it has something to do with the position of the head and a curling of the lips at the end of the phrase, something I call a grimace because it's a public face made for an audience, like the faces on the prows of boats, parting rivers and oceans with their unique scowls—with that face, I turn to Valfrido, who's sweeping the clippings of his last clients and punctuating Osvaldo's monologue with discordant grunts. I look in the mirror at him, behind me, where new strands now fall, to be swept up by his broom, and I recall Ritinha, at the end of the day, sweeping the trimmings from the sewing room's wine-colored linoleum.

I'd get home from the bank at nearly six and had an hour to eat and study before leaving for night school. The house was in chaos—kids taking baths, mother preparing dinner, father arriving in silence and settling among his papers, setting the mood for the rest of the house. I would go to the sewing room to do my homework. Ritinha unplugged the radio when she heard me coming. She swept with a soft-bristled broom, softly humming the rest of the interrupted song. Twice a week she went to her typing course and the other three nights she took classes in design. The broom and her hips both moved to the rhythm of the music, her flesh firm, swaying with the sweeping. She wore striped dresses, long and modest. The skirts swished across the back of her thighs as she shifted her weight from one leg to the other, the scraps and clippings fluttering with the breeze before they were swept into a tangle of black threads. She was a cheerful girl, and always wore a thick coiled braid in the daytime, hours which for her passed easily, vespers to the night—when her life really began. She liked everyone and was a quick study: she hemmed, sewed, embroidered, took measurements, cut patterns, helped around the house, swept up, smiled and played along. We were too little to be of any use. Despite the distraction, I still managed to study, not with any absorption, but in a way that lent itself to humming, hips, the swish of the broom, the verb connecting to its indirect object, the wars and revolts and phagocytosis, the process by which a cell or a group of cells will incorporate solid particles, engulfing them, a process that does not require the penetration of a cellular membrane and which acts as a means of nutrition and defense against foreign elements within an organism. The difficult part was the sequence of bending, showering, see-you-in-the-morning. The bending part is obvious: when the girl is young, and the boy watching is young too, she doesn't kneel down, but keeps her legs straight and bends her body down, swaying as she brushes the scraps into the dustpan. Then came her shower in the tiny bathroom behind the sewing room, where everything was thrown together on top of everything else: cold shower, sink, and toilet. No steam—just the smell of soap and a song that had regained its lyrics, under the false protection of a sheet of plywood that barely functioned as a door. It only blocked the view, which made matters worse. I plugged my ears but the melody was already inside, hammering away, thumping my stomach and regions south. And the variation of the rhythm corresponded to the changes in the sound of the water, which sometimes nearly stopped: rinsing here, then over there, a little more here, water spilling across, my God, wherever her hand was lathering. When she finished, she turned off the tap—the lyrics faded once more and all that remained was a melody that drifted away as she concentrated on drying the enormous surfaces and curves and the spaces between her fingers, between everything, the brush in her hair and now her clothes, and then the plywood door opens. Sweating and drained, I laugh awkwardly as Rita the typist and designer emerges, hair hanging in lose waves, her dress low-necked and tight-waisted, the skirt to her knee, lipstick on her lips, see you tomorrow buddy, I'm going to class.

But the only thing that changes is the date on the stamp. In my research at the lab, even that didn't change. For days and months it was always the same cell structures that, it's true, are born, die, reproduce, and everything else: a productive life, varied and dynamic, but alway the same. It was an exasperating routine, doing the same thing for eight hours a day—I couldn't take it. I compared it to the courses I taught in college prep and felt like I was wasting time. But I learned to describe what I observed with precision. Describing is sharing, inserting an observation into the chain of common knowledge, with its need for precision, for established nomenclature and recognizable methodology. The trouble is that every discipline has its own specific procedures, created according to its needs. And I'm not referring to the theoretical bias of a particular school, but to the slice of reality that each branch of knowledge sets out to capture. This slice obliges us to use a certain language, to establish its names and necessary procedures so that through it we can get *closer*. There's already a story in motion, its false starts and deviations the result of ancient battles that today are meaningless, but language continues to carry the names we are in fact obliged to use if we wish to have our thoughts included in the common chain.

I wasn't trained for any special chain, I was never part of any of the organizations, and I had to guess at the correct discourse. There, more than in any other space of knowledge, speech is reality: it creates and modifies, kills and saves.

It's a pity
What a pity
the way a poor heart suffers
its only relief is to tell everyone
the thing that nobody says.

Jose would say, Luiza said, Eliana suffered, Dona Esther died. I'm not acquainted with this relief, nor its necessity. It's a paraphrase that's worse than bad, it's inadequate, José. I couldn't just make something up because I knew I wouldn't be able to remember what I said, and the incoherence of my story could get Armando killed. I always knew those were the stakes. But, I repeat, I had not been trained. For the suffering, the physical pain, we all are, or aren't—anyway, it wasn't going to be some gang of idiots who made me capable of withstanding mutilation, much less the idea of a mission I valued above life. Fucking life. This is something they never understood, especially you, José—by this point you were off smoking pot in Caixa Prego. The moral necessity, the feeling of loyalty and compassion, the colossal force that sweeps us up and compels us to resist adversity—it has nothing to do with adherence to missions or responsibility or a better future or being the protagonist of History or—*what, my God?* "I have ever hated all nations, professions, and communities and all my love is toward individuals," Swift said, and I've always felt the same.

I found out later that the organization had rules about what to say and when to say it once someone is captured. If people "fell," they needed to resist for a few days in silence, after which it wouldn't be so serious if they gave up addresses and names, because the information would already be useless. There were other things that could be divulged during torture sessions, given that talking was necessary to avoid being killed: tell them whatever they want to hear, buy time for the machine to be disassembled and for your comrades to go into hiding. They started by saying what was already "in the open," merely confirming what the soldiers already knew, making subsequent depositions seem credible, feeding their torturers a few valid facts, as though they were already giving in—and then, between useless facts, the names and addresses of idiots like me, people who knew nothing and who would certainly be released when it turned out they had a solid alibi. But I didn't know any of this and, beneath the blows, I tried to keep guessing at the language, the codes and procedures.

Armando was a good militant and, in spite of our close friendship—in truth, because of it—he never told me anything about his activities. The torturers already knew much more than me. Armando had participated in a kidnapping and a bank robbery, he'd laundered money, prepared safe houses for fugitives. The part about safe houses I knew. Later I found out the rest was just as true. In our apartment we took in a lowlife from Rio Grande do Sul whose nom de guerre was Joyce. He tried to seduce Eliana and all her friends. After I became a deaf widower, I learned that I could have said anything I knew—Armando would not have been affected by my words.

Alexandre was here to take a look at my computer. It might've caught a virus. The internet is slow, it comes and goes, and I haven't received a single email. Cecília didn't confirm receipt of the material I sent, and it's been two days since I've seen any ads for penis enlargement. Alexandre lives next door and brings his furry dog along with him. While he examines the various connections between the processor, printer, CD drive, and modem, he explains the correct pedagogy for training dogs. I go to the next room, start reading something that's doomed by his interruptions to incompletion. There's no escape: he needs to tell me about the dog, which is really quite nice, about the thousand dangers of not putting a password on everything, about the way the hackers can get in and screw up your whole life, enough horrors to make me want to give up on the computer and go back to my typewriter. I made the switch to a computer when Renato came to live with us. While he was still alive, he showed me the basics and fixed any sort of problem I ran into. The truth is that he managed to captivate me. I regret the foolish accident, and the argument we had before it.

I like Alexandre. I like his misanthropic dedication to dogs. I distract myself these lonely days with something or another. São Paulo and São Carlos, teacher and retired. Lígia and her family took a trip to avoid the holiday bustle in the city. She prefers to take her summer vacation in December and work through January, when São Paulo resumes a semblance of civility for thirty days. She said she's coming back in time for Christmas. She doesn't need to, not on my account any-way, but she says she wants to spend one last Christmas at 7 Vaz Leme. Jussara and José are coming, too. I'm the one who would prefer to leave. I'm not in the family Christmas habit. But leaving would be an aggressive way to manage my feelings and besides, I miss Marta. She calls me *Grumps*, she's already talking and everything, and she loves coming here to the house. We go berry-picking. She eats some, scowls with comical exaggeration when she gets a bitter one, and later smashes them into the dirt. She mixes them with water and leaves, and plays at making potions. We end up covered in mud and berry juice. I show her how to find pill bugs and pop the buds on hostas. I wanted Lígia to move to São Carlos. Alexandre's dog shed all over the place and I sneezed through the night. I need to remember to sweep and wipe up with a damp cloth. Vanise can tell as soon as she steps foot in the house that Alexandre was here. She comes every Thursday, cleans, does the laundry, bakes some cornbread, and mostly keeps to herself. She hardly says anything. Alexandre and his dog are one of the few subjects we discuss.

The guy is down, the guy is down.
Down, down, down, he's wasted, down and out.
The guy's uncle comes in, gets right up in his face and says:
done, done, done, you've really done it now, no, no, no, no.
The guy turns to his uncle, says: you're dumb, dum-dum-dum,
a dummy with no money, you just work, work, work,
you work day and night, night and day, you're never done,
you drag ourself home and drink yourself dumb.
Then the dumb guy's daughter, who's the down guy's cousin,
she comes running, running down, running dumb,
so she doesn't have to listen to the dumb drunks chatter.
And then her grandma, who's nothing to the cousin,
from a good family, goody-goody, there she is,
tec-tec-tec, tock-tock-tock, seam in the front, seam in the back,
back to front, front to back,
knead the dough and sew and fold
and everything's fine, fine-fine-fine.
There's no problem, just solution,
leave the boy, don't tease your uncle, let's go eat,
hey, hey, I'm on top, hey, hey, hey.
Tits on her, ass on him, but she doesn't let her cuz's hand slip
    down to the pet
between her thighs, she never smelled or felt so good,
in her pits, her neck, her puss.
Oui, oui, oui, mon oncle, just like that
I'm done, totally done, over there and down,
I'm almost done.
And the test is gonna come, and this guy's gotta hit the books,
and he's no down-done-don, cuz he knows how to hustle.
Mon oncle, monocle. One big eye, just one,
that stares into faces, gazes out at the world,
doesn't glance at the tits on the miss or mommy's tic-tic-tock,
one big tired eye, grey, it wants to swallow me, single me out.

Get outta this fool, no gutter punk ass, or your uncle's clean.
Spick-and-span, Johnson's baby.
Uncle hasn't fucked in more than a year.
Tired of the girls' "teacher, teacher," uncle's bone's gone dry.
What's that dum-dum, you gonna tell me that you get it up?
What's worse, unc, never having what they want or beating
  off all alone.
Teacher, teacher, put it right there, oh!—
rub my tits like this, lick my pussy like that.
And teach just stands there in his boxers.
The guy wears boxers. How's he even do it?
And that cousin of Basílio's gives it up,
Capitú gives it up, I only gotta study for the entrance exam.
Done done, dom dom.

Renato—notebook, circa 1987

Renato's two obsessions: sex and the computer. Conversation was impossible, not for lack of topics, but his hunger irritated me. He was an opinionated boy. He was ready with commentary on the direct elections, Tancredo Neves, Ulysses Guimarães, José Sarney, the constituent assembly, the cruzado. It was a tumultuous time and he wanted to talk. I don't know why it was so difficult for me to listen. He was so vague, exhibitionist, emotional. His age: I was used to it from being in the schools, the university, but in him I couldn't accept it. Always adjusting his crotch and ravenous for women. He was a good student, with his father's intelligence and natural ability. How would Armando have dealt with a boy like this? Maybe Renato wouldn't be this way if he'd had a father. The family curse of fatherless boys. With the computer between us, we understood one another: he was the teacher, and a good one at that. He enjoyed the subject. That's really all it takes: enjoying the subject. You don't even have to like the student, because sufficient passion for mathematics includes enjoying the challenge of infecting others with that passion. It never entered Renato's mind that I might not be aroused for every single second of my classes: not to admit to an overflowing sexual desire for every one of the three hundred pretty girls passing through my classrooms every year would make me a complete hypocrite. Now that seems funny, but then it turned my stomach, beholding this transformation of woman into female, an object of the hunt. Renato argued that they did the same thing, that they felt the same desire. That it was just good fun for everybody. Animals—peacocks, wolves, hyenas. Didn't I see?

But with the computer everything went fine. He taught me how to use spreadsheets and the word processor. He enjoyed it and I needed to learn the basics. We sometimes ask ourselves how to create this feeling of need—the need for formal knowledge among our students. But shouldn't we be asking how to create a passion for the material (and not for instruction) in the teacher? It's not for nothing that researchers are, generally speaking, better teachers than the nonresearchers. Teaching should be that space where knowledge overflows from other activities. And the overflowing then would be joyous, committed, and demanding. The students become interlocutors and partners in a process linked to life, not one closed in on itself.

> *I had a history teacher who was a real piece of work, a specialist in Euclides da Cunha. During our classes he was constantly writing articles for the* Estadão, *always about Euclides da Cunha. I remember something unusual: he wrote with a green pen, with green ink. His class went like this: he called on the first and second in the class—there was a boy called Aquiles*

who was the best one—"Number one"—but I don't remember
the name of the second-best one. "Number one," he'd say, act-
ing as though he didn't know it was Aquiles, "read from page
such and such of Joaquim da Silva," the author of the textbook
he used. And the kid would start reading and he would go on
writing, and this was history class in the best public high school
in São Paulo.

Someone like me—*recent conversation*

One-on-one teaching doesn't always yield the best results. But my lessons with Renato were excellent and from him I learned the essentials for managing machines: the problem, uncle, is that the computer doesn't do what you want it to do, only what you tell it to do. Teachers, in a school, never do what the principal tells them, only what they want. Any change in procedure has to take their desires into account, something I think I usually do pretty well.

The word "uncle" was banished. A false and lazy intimacy, clouding each of our roles, teacher and student.

Unlike José, I obviously hold on to all of my notes and documents. Even now, with digital backups, I only trust printed paper. And now I have to deal with this mountain of folders and carloads of books that will certainly never fit in the little house that's waiting in São Carlos. After the hustle-bustle of goodbyes, honors, and finishing up my courses—and before the beginning of a new apprenticeship: a new job, new house, new neighborhood and city—I find myself wading through the echoing void I came to know when they let me out of prison. It lacks the despair of those times, but it's sad just the same. Back then, like now, the world had lost its clarity and I fumbled along, trying to relocate my place in the world and feel out a future trajectory that could pull me from the void. I started to work like a madman. I still always get up early, I don't know how not to. I go out for the newspaper and my bread, and lately, I prefer to drink my coffee right there in the bakery. Its difficult to face down a whole day without arguments, without decisions to make, pressures to manage, human contact.

Topics under discussion at the bakery might change with the times, but soccer is a constant. I root for Santos, but I never really followed the game that closely. Armando and Eliana rooted for São Paulo, but nobody at home really cared much either way. Only after I was older, over twenty, did I begin to go with Armando to see games at a stadium. Although his team was São Paulo, he never missed a Santos game. It was impossible not to admire that team in the Sixties. Sometimes we'd go to Vila Belmiro stadium. Eliana liked going, too. I transformed myself, not exactly into a fanatic, but certainly into an enthusiast. Eliana found the game beautiful. She enjoyed watching the fans react and cheer, but never got to the point of understanding the championship brackets, or keeping up with the scuttlebutt. Armando used to read the sports section before anything else, and his mood varied tremendously according to the scores. He waxed philosophical about the matches, read interviews with players, and kept up with their lives. He had an excellent memory, and was the kind of guy who could tell rattle off the entire São Paulo roster for the past however-many years. I didn't go to such lengths. I still read the news first, but I knew how the season was going for Santos, the names of the players, things like that. Then it happened. Life and Santos changed. Two years ago our beachfront team started to shine again and I perceived, in the bakery, for instance, that saying Santos was my team is no longer seen as some kind of shame or irony. I started reading the sports section again.

This morning the professor said that in '73 we were Paulista champions, still with Pelé. It's strange how in my mind, part of reality, some of its flux, was interrupted after 1970. The professor has his blanks, too: immense clouds that carry him off to a peaceful place, I think, because he appears calm during these absences. The other regulars at the bakery consider him just another neighborhood character. He was a literature professor, he activated the electric connections necessary for the enjoyment of writing in hundreds or thousands of nervous systems still young enough to be connected. Recently something in his mind was disconnected—an aneurism or something like that. He retired and sometimes wanders around the neighborhood, talking to strangers, reciting lines from the *Lusíadas* in a voice that's still strong. I don't know how, but the bakery cashiers know his story, they treat him well, but the other customers are perturbed by his praises of their eyes or bodies, made without any moderation to his affect. The professor sits at a little booth near the counter, turns to a girl and says, your eyes are so pretty, and then he forgets himself, his mind lost in admiration of the girl. Along with his short-term memory, he lost the awareness and self-control required for social life. But he's kind in these moments, and his admiration for the girls is so sincere that I don't think he runs a risk beyond the occasional tart reply.

In my case, perceptions about which flows had been interrupted were delayed. I refer not to memory loss, although that has happened, as well, if on a lesser scale. First came a loss of perception, the perception of reality—or of interest in reality, which ends up being the same thing. Music and soccer, for example. The Seventies are one big blank. Not that I know much about what came later, but I have vague memories of specific games, the names of some players, and certain

84

melodies. Literature, poetry, cinema, art, theater: nothing happened for ten years. After 1980 the fog begins to dissipate and some shapes become perceptible, but it's a distant realm that I couldn't reach, even if I had the interest. What's missing? I read the classics, some for the first time. A few years ago I began to curate a small collection of my favorite records, this time on CD, even though I still haven't managed to get rid of my LPs and my father's ancient victrola. Lígia gave me a CD player as a gift, and some nights I listen to music. Sometimes I go out with my friends to bars that play old samba. On my Sunday strolls I end up, eventually, at a museum, or see gallery shows. I read the reviews of new books. I go to the cinema, sometimes I like a new film. Yes, the funk of interest is re-forming, but something changed. Maybe it's my age, or the world, or a combination of the two.

A distracted perception of art. The prose of my students' mothers, gossip from around the neighborhood, the bakery, the university. And politics, which I took to reading about in the newspaper as though it were a soap opera—it had acquired the same weight as a book or a film. All of it fleeting and light. My studies, my linguistic research saved me from this lethargy and alienation—only work mattered. Mobilizing people for action, forming part of a group, taking care of those around me, placing myself in the line of fire: after prison that was how I lived in public and at school. Then I immersed myself in my studies at the university. Now I want to reread this Brazilian novel and listen to that Brazilian song and see another Brazilian film, but the meanings have changed, and I can't find what I'm looking for.

I must be deafer, or perhaps older, than I realize, because every book I pick up, every song, every painting seems part of one vast adolescent phase, even the theses and essays and debates over politics and public education. I can't help feeling like I lost the ability to see the world with foreign eyes. It's true that Diego and Robinho, Renato, Maurinho and Alberto, Alex and André Luiz managed to do this at the end of 2002. Not that bastard Fábio Costa who went and lost the championship game of the Libertadores cup to a bunch of Argentine punks. The professor corrects me, recalling that Costa saved the day in the final against Corinthans. But soccer is another story, almost like sex.

In today's teacher training, we discussed the importance of valorizing oral production in school and distinguishing the difference between oral and written codes. Helena, a Portuguese teacher in public high school, told us about a class she'd taught on argumentative texts. She proposed a fictional situation in which there would be a referendum in Brazil, to approve or reject the death penalty. She explained to the students what a referendum was and told them that to imagine they were being paid to write a pamphlet on the subject. Each group had to write a a text to convince the other voters of their point of view, for or against.

Helena explained that she began the class with a conversation about which arguments might be raised against one side or the other. As the students spoke, the teacher wrote their comments on the board. She explained the idea of a counterargument, an argument that serves as response to another view that it presupposes. She explained the appeal to authority and other types of argumentative strategies, which the students then discussed. The discussion became heated and everyone participated, sometimes aggressively. Helena showed them that argumentative strategies such as shouting, threatening, and physical aggression have no place in a written text where only words have power, and for this reason their thoughts needed to be carefully arranged to be convincing. Other strategies that might work well during an interpersonal exchange, like weeping or other manipulations, would need to be formulated in some other way in a third-person text, in which the author and the audience remain anonymous.

When the arguments had all been discussed, explained, and written on the board, the groups began to write their texts. The class calmed and finally started talking about how to write. After a while, the student who had been the biggest cheerleader for the death penalty indignantly shouted, "It's not fair! We got stuck being the bad guys, the ones who want to kill people! It's a lot easier to be against it and be the nice guy." Helena tells us that she only laughed and was pleased her student had realized the "importance and responsibility that words possess."

Myself—*professional development course,* 2001

The tales of a time when novels and films could change the world strike me as curious. First the world existed to be praised in song: wars were waged so they could be narrated, but after centuries and millennia had passed the song became a weapon. A real weapon, with a trigger and an explosion. Reality is not transformed within the work of art, it's transformed by the work. Each reader, spectator, or listener becomes an armed agent of the transformation. It was more or less at such a time that I was apprehended, released, and stopped paying attention.

I worked and studied a lot in those ten years in which I didn't watch any soccer. I was transferred from school to school, I did my master's, my doctorate, I started lecturing at the university. I returned to my need for an exact description, of gathering what's already been thought out and settled, and then advancing with small, sure steps. And fear, an enormous fear hovered in the air, a dense and colorless smoke separated us, controlling all speech, containing only simple pleasantries. A collective gushing. Cursed, ten thousand times cursed. I don't know if anyone today has any idea of what the fear was like. The humiliation of fear. The only excess was rage. That's why there's nostalgia for time we had a common enemy. Those who don't remember can't discern the horror of the word *common*. We were in common with the enemy: it was a part of us, among us: we were one with it, because of it. The beatings, shocks, the night raids became medals of honor and merit. Precisely because we were beaten, we continue to be those who were never beaten.

Helena's cheer was excessive. She is serious, and she's right. I'm an old crank who mixes apples and oranges, and the joy that Helena took in the "responsibility that words possess" seems almost frivolous to me. In bed I hear Eliana's voice, and it calms me. Lígia is now older than Eliana ever was. Renato never reached his father's age. Renato died drunk when he drove his car into a post. If Eliana had been alive she certainly would have known how to prevent my confrontation with Renato. Not in the way that Dona Joana had done, protecting the father from sons and sons from father. Actually she never did this, it's a lie from José's book that's wormed its way in and frozen a certain story in place, one that isn't mine. Joaquim Ferreira didn't need protection from anybody and he never threatened us. I admired him, I wanted his silence in me, without any of our mother's confusing chatter. Dona Joana was nosy and barged into every space. She had no patience for masculine hesitation. She was what we might call a "facilitator" today. Because teachers, today, they don't teach anymore: they facilitate, stimulate, and organize the process. They lubricate, oil, grease, smooth, sand. Lubricious, slippery, lustrous, sheened, penetration without pain. Screwy words, screwy images. And Helena is serious, yes, I know. Poor Dona Joana, she wouldn't like to see herself inserted in this rigamarole. And Grandma Ana, back then, the teacher of so many boys and girls who remained grateful to her their entire lives: they wrote to her on her birthday, they sent her postcards. But Dona Ana, she didn't teach anything, she only facilitated the process. *Of course*, my grandmother would say: her straightforwardness was light-years ahead of my screwy senilities.

But now, in this intermission in life, Eliana has been visiting me more often. Just now, Lígia was teaching Marta that after death our bodies are eaten by bugs. She laughs and tells her friends, by way of explanation, about the strange education she'd received, our sunny strolls between the tombs and the grave we made for her mother—just now Eliana's spirit visits me and calms me. She was always sweet and soft, but has become more cheerful in old age. She's no longer frightened by my outbursts: she even finds them funny. Sometimes she treats me like a child. And with her I'm able to laugh at my rages and accept time as a passive assistant: passively I watch and wait, and time goes on without my help. It's not hypocrisy or indifference, or irresponsibility, she says: it's stepping aside, making space, having patience, knowing when you can't do everything, being ready, staying close. Little, feminine things like that, perhaps a bit timid, but maybe they'd have helped me avoid a conflict that proved insufferable. Who knows.

I'd never seen this notebook of Renato's before. I found it when I was clearing things out for the move. I need to give it to Luiza. I was going to say give it back to her, but it was never hers, nor mine. Returning is an act of giving back something lent or forgotten. Who owns Renato? The dead never forget these things. Anyway, I place *return* in the same classification as reply, respond, refuse. I don't even know where Luiza is anymore, she vanished. And this time I refuse nothing. I don't even know what I'm talking about. I never refused. It's just that sometimes I had the impression that Luiza saddled me with Renato as a punishment, a debt that fell to me to honor. In school I always had more patience with adolescents. Maybe that's not the right word. They require certain things and my hearing had been altered. In the professional development courses, I get a glimpse into how things have changed over the past fifteen years. The responsibilities of teachers and principals are different, and what families and society expect from the schools has changed. In the shift from teacher to educator, the operational elements are inverted: school as extension of family became family as extension of school—today's schools require educating the parents.

Eliana graduated early and then we got married. At one point I'll have to stop and put all these old things in order. To think: Eliana as an old thing. These papers I find tucked away in closets and drawers. Our father died, then mother, Renato. Lígia moved, Jussara married, each one leaving behind bills, letters, checkbooks, minutes of meetings, notebooks, everything worn at the edges. If the house weren't going to be demolished it would all stay right here until the next resident threw them out. The painter, the cabinetmaker, the foreman, or maybe Tobias: they'd come prepare a new home in the house, they'd replace the old pipes, the wires, maybe change the tiles, so worn down that they're no longer level. A new coat of paint on the walls, varnish on the closet doors, and all these papers would go down to the dumpster.

I have my systems, I always have: in school, at the university, at home. They're idiosyncratic—all of ours are—but perfectly intelligible to anyone who needs to consult them. My advisees, for instance: after a few months they'd already be able to find any book, thesis, or journal in my office. The lazy ones could never find them, they'd accuse me of being messy or of purposefully creating codes revealed only to my disciples.Vile infamies (redundancy of emphasis) of indolent minds. Each person is a new theory of knowledge. Understanding his systems of organization for anything—books, clothing, relationships—means getting to know him. It's something I've always been curious about. But now, during this tail-end to the year, and retired, I wonder if I should bother trying to know, or continue knowing, those who are dead and gone. Papers and more papers. Dona Joana's patterns, Grandma Ana's school notes, old man Joaquim's drafts of minutes and manifestoes, Jussara's letters, Lígia's stories, notes, and outlines; and José's book. Cecília would be interested in all this. Fragments of life in no particular order, awaiting imagination, or a necessity, or whatever might sew them together.

My father had his first stroke while I was in prison and died a few months later. My mother told me he was furious with Armando. I rarely saw my father furious. He grumbled, there was a lot he didn't like, especially a lack of objectivity or anything whimsical. Politics isn't for putting your feet up and feeling fine, it's not a way of gaining friends. It's only a way of obtaining things: simple, shared things—improvements to salary, working conditions, family benefits—or so my father, Joaquim Ferreria, would say. He wasn't in love with Jango and he didn't despair the coup. I don't know if his love was limited to individuals, but he distrusted the powerful and all their institutions. They were his adversaries and so he had to understand their mechanisms. It seems he wasn't a good negotiator, or at least that's what Francisco Augusto told me—he was close to the postal workers during the social movements. My father was not on the front line, swept along by the current of national politics: that was something of which he disapproved.

But, Francisco Augusto tells me, his legacy remained alive and they consulted him when they needed to mobilize the old guard. My father knew more about movements and organizations than I did. After the coup, he became even more closed-off and left his post at the union. He stopped bringing home all those papers. I didn't witness this phase: I'd already left home. One day, after his death, I asked Francisco Augusto what my father's position had been with regard to the movements. He was evasive. He said that old man Joaquim only spoke about internal problems at the Post Office. But I know that he and Armando had had a serious disagreement. I thought maybe Armando had stuck his nose into union politics. But maybe that confuses things, because around the time I started college and José left home, my father no longer cared for Armando, and the meatballs had returned to being meatballs. They were no longer "Armando's."

The fact is that the old man, in his more active days, would keep quiet in the assemblies and the meetings with the bosses. If asked, he would advise the leadership in short sentences, uttered in a low voice. This agrees with what I remember of the nighttime meetings at our house. He would laugh at jokes, he liked hearing the cases members brought to be discussed, and he told his own, too. But he he didn't get swept up in any excitement. He waited for the silence and then summarized all the shouting in two or three sentences: the positions advanced during the past two hours are this-and-that and such-and-such. I was reminded of him when I watched the *Great Dictator*, during the scene in which Chaplin's Hitler barks out pseudo-German, and then the English translation of his words. After a long speech full of howls and grunts, the translator explains in half a second: the führer has expressed his feelings in relation to the Jewish people. Now I look through his papers and the printed materials from the union. In his careful handwriting I find a list of items on a half page of cheap paper. The same items appear on a printed page in the form of a page-long manifesto, front and back, written by a colleague, inflated with patriotic vehemence. The rhetoric of words invoking order not only offended my father's sensibilities: more importantly, they insulted his ideology, which he claimed not to have. He disagreed with any use of patriotism, nationalism, or internationalism. He had trouble with the idea of uniting students, blue collar laborers, peasants, and the proletariat. His universe was that of the manual laborers, farmhands, sharecroppers, squatters, factory workers, public servants. There was no united front, only interior, outback, farm, plantation.

> *Two large puddles formed on the the edges of the roof where it sagged from the weight, a tenement for trolls and pigmies: behind and to the left of the drooping avocado tree was my mother's sewing shed. On the right, a fragrant pitanga tree that hid the clothesline and the washtub. The veranda was an addition made of corrugated metal with an earthen floor. Two plastic wires, black and red, made languid love to three naked bulbs. Inside, mother and grandma put up lampshades, but in the veranda it was a matter of hanging them and waiting for our father to unscrew them and toss them aside. Then Joana would replace them, saying, this time leave it, because without it I can't see straight. At a loss, my father unscrews it, removes it, walks away, tosses it aside.*

> José—*unpublished manuscript*

At a loss of what, José? Each one us is so full of things. For my father to solicit the words then and clean them up, holding his tongue was essential. This wasn't a loss or some kind of negligence—only my brother's blindness. Every utterance was a ready-made thing. He never learned to soliloquize, he either argued or ridiculed—a light joke, a heavy one, he knew how to rise to the occasion, so long as no one expected anything long and drawn out. That was an apprenticeship we undertook with our mother and Grandma Ana. Both ways of talking are complete: the word that's made and the word that's in the making. Our mother was a bit of a gossip, a habit among those who work with their hands. Grandma Ana on the other hand was more cautious. She liked to listen and work with words, but not in the weighty way our father did. Like anything placed in the world for all to see, she took care that her words would turn out nice.

—*You there, Dona Joana? And Dona Ana?*
Our singsong Bahian neighbor came calling at the end of each year to ask my mother's permission to take some branches from the pitanga tree. They lived in back of a house three doors down and didn't have space for any plants. Her daughter was a neighborhood friend of mine: a pretty girl with a strong temper and braids, scraggly thin. Hey, son, where's Dona Ana? Their place was on the second floor of a shack, just a single room with a stove in one corner, a bed in another, and a table in the middle with four little benches underneath. A patterned curtain, red with yellow flowers, hid the toilet and shower. Where do you and Nico sleep, I asked Zininha. When she bent down to show me a mattress under her parents bed, I could see her underwear, smeared with mud. I thought about Zininha and Nico sleeping in that tiny little space under the boobs, butt, and arms of Dona

Iracy and her husband. Dona Ana, who was in from São Carlos for the holidays, was reading the newspaper, ironing clothes, straightening her grandchildren's beds, picking beans, reading a novel, listening to the radio, hoeing the garden, clearing undergrowth, hanging things to dry, making pitanga jelly and arrowroot cookies, darning socks—anything that made her feel like less of a burden in our house, and also to pass the time—nothing she couldn't interrupt just like that to chew the fat, her face cheerful and full of apologies for being so useless.

—Oh, Dona Ana, do you think this year Dona Joana could spare some pitanga branches for our New Year?

—Dona Iracy, come on in, I was just about to put some coffee on.

—Oh, I couldn't Dona Ana, I couldn't, I don't want to be a bother. If Dona Joana is with a client, I'll come back later.

She started to turn around, pulling her kids down from the post at the gate. They never came inside our house. Donana knew this, but insisted anyway. Even the children couldn't come in. Only the yard and the veranda, which had a dirt floor. They never set foot in the house. I went into their home whenever I wanted: it held some kind of fascination for me, I'd go for no other reason than to be in a place so full and alive, warm with so many things, dimly lit, the floors cool. There was only one door and a ventilation window with milky glass that tipped outward. Their room was above the workshop of an old cobbler, Mr. Jonas, who lived in the house in front. At five o'clock in the afternoon they'd light the oil lamp—that was when I most liked to be there, amid the strong smell of people and kerosene. Zininha had a rag doll. Grandma Ana made a boy doll for me. I'd take some of my mother's fabric scraps and we'd play for hours, climbing on the bed, the benches, and the table, jumping on top, stuffing ourselves under the bed, whispering our fears about the monsters who peered out at us from the fireplace or from behind the red curtain. They'd grow and grow, becoming terribly large and cruel, hating children more and more, ready to sniff us out. Zininha's scent: acrid and wet. She let out a wet laugh, her lips wet, her eyes wet with excitement about the monster. She cowered up against me.

—What are they going to do?

—They'll come slowly, shuffling their feet so that we can't hear them get closer. They're going to crouch down and reach under here.

And Zininha would throw herself against me with excitement and fear, curl up behind my back, so that she'd be protected from the terrible hand that was approaching:

—No! Their hands are too fat, they won't fit under here.

—Silly girl, they just stay out there and wait, all they need is a little piece of your dress and woosh! *they'll pull you out. And you know what happens then.*

A nervous laugh.

—Tell me.

—First they smell you all over, just like this.

And I sniff Zininha with loud grunts like an evil monster. She laughs and pushes me away.

—And then they start to taste your skin in little bites, to see which parts are the best. They take a little lick and then a little nibble, a lick and a nibble, just like big kitten.

And I'd go slowly. Zininha was ticklish, she'd laugh and flail in all directions.

—Look out, Zininha, your leg is sticking out! Look—here comes the hairy monster's hand!

She'd scream in terror and scrunch up behind me again.

—And then what? Tell me what else.

—And then, Zininha, something awful happens.

—What is it?

—I can't tell you. If I do, you'll scream and cry and it will ruin everything.

—I promise I won't.

*—All right. Well, then, Zininha, they rip off one of your arms—*humfch, chrumf, murunch*—they tear out your bones and rip your muscles apart in their hands and then lick up all the blood that spurts out. And they get smeared with your blood, and splinters of your bones get stuck in their thick fur as they chew up and swallow your whole arm. After that they come up to your ear like this and suck on it so hard that it pulls everything out from inside, your eyes, your teeth, your tongue, just like that.*

Zininha squeals when I press my mouth up to her ear. One time, she bit me hard on the cheek. I howl from the pain and she escapes from under the bed. I chase her down the stairs and takes off onto the street. Dona Iracy is coming home, and her daughter skips in after her like nothing happened, helping her mother with her bags. I have time to hide in Mr. Jonas's workshop while the two of them go upstairs. Zininha sees me from the corner of her eye and sticks out her tongue, swinging her shoulders.

—Dona Iracy, come back. Dona Joana's out making a delivery. But of course you can take some branches.

—No, thank you, Dona Ana. I appreciate it, but I'd rather wait for her. It's better that way, right? There's no hurry. It's not New Year's Eve yet.

—Dona Iracy, don't be stubborn, come here woman, and trim that tree—the fruit's already gone. Son, go inside and get the garden shears and climb up in the tree where I tell you.

I was there, hiding behind my grandmother's skirt, waiting for a solution to this feminine impasse. Dona Iracy was saying, no, no, what's the hurry? Grandma Ana was insisting we do it right then—go on, son, are you deaf? They go back and forth and don't get anywhere.

—When Dona Joana gets home I'll come back and Nico will climb the tree, he's done it before, look at him, he's like a monkey, never stays put on the ground. Hey, kid, get down from the gate, you hear? Sit still for a minute, Mother Mary, if this doesn't stop, just look at his leg, it didn't heal right.

My father appeared at the end of the street. Dona Iracy was in a hurry to gather her chicks and get going. She had the chest and the butt of a brooding hen, and her chicks tottered along behind. But leaving without saying hello would be rude. My father was timid, but with a broad smile he smoothed Zininha's hair and stuck his hand out for Dona Iracy.

—Joaquim, our neighbor needs some pitanga branches for her New Year's party.

—Oh, it's not a party, Dona Ana, we're too poor for that kind of luxury, it's just to have a pleasant smell in the doorway. Good afternoon, sir, I don't want to be a bother, I was just going, I'll come back later.

—"It's no trouble at all.

They were already moving inside, shooing Nico and Zininha along.

—"Son, run inside and get the garden shears and cut some branches with new leaves, they have a better smell.

I brought the shears but didn't want to go up the tree. I knew how to climb, I even enjoyed it, but I didn't want to do it with my father watching, and certainly not the pitanga tree, which had high, thin branches that were difficult to climb. I was shy and self-conscious about my awkwardness as a fat kid. My father knew it but he didn't perceive depth of my shame. Or he discerned it and took it upon himself to teach me a lesson in front of the neighbors, fortify my character, and get me to snap out of this spoiled-child routine. He was so cavalier about something so minor to him and so enormously major to me that I burned

inside, turned red, and swore I wouldn't do it. Twiggy Nico, ready to climb, stopped himself when he saw my father's stern gaze. Sensing that the situation had taken a serious turn, Dona Iracy wanted to flee the scene, but didn't dare say a word. Unlike the desires of the women in the house, my father's weren't divulged with words. I couldn't look him in the eye and neither of us spoke. But I felt his gaze boring into my head as I stared at his dusty shoes and the thunder of his anger and disappointment. Amado was looking down and laughing from the window in our room. He came bounding down, took the shears from my hands and climbed to the very top of the tree. Freed, I ran inside blindly to my room to smash my face into the pillow and smother my screaming hate. G. was studying at the desk behind the door.
—Shut up, faggot.

Under the pillow, little by little, I let it all out. I bit the pillowcase so that no one could hear me, my heart pounding as the tears streamed from my eyes, clenched with rage. But after a while it was all gone. It made me tired, weak, the voice of my father directing Amado to the best branches seemed far away, sweet and deep. I was the one in the tree and my father was happy with my fearlessness, easily accomplishing his orders. Everyone was laughing at Amado's monkeyish stunts in the tree, even our father was laughing. Even our father. Zininha was me, whom you watched with laughter, it was me who pretended I was going to fall before flipping off a branch onto the ground. I went to the window to look out, and I laughed, too. I went back down and helped Zininha and Nico gather the branches from the ground.

José—*unpublished manuscript*

When we're little, the weakness of others is profoundly irritating. We cant't admit that it's not some kind of stratagem, a wily way of getting something that might require too much honest effort. Artifice, like fireworks. Fire that is not fire, imitation. Imitation is not being—it's something else with no relation to the original. It enchants. It enchants because it perverts and transforms. We can no longer discern the lie. A liar, whoever says that verisimilitude and fraud are unrelated. José lies flagrantly when he describes what he was, what we were. He lies, but it's him, it's really him, that boy who won't climb the pintanga tree and later makes his glorious ascent in the body of his imaginary brother Amado. An invention, this boy who doesn't have a shred of courage to approach a girl, but who, in the guise of a monster, will suck her brains out. I'm the one who says shut up, faggot. He does what I say. Boys, when we're young, confuse femininity with weakness. We allow girls to be treated differently: she's a girl, soft, prissy, dissembling. It's like that: full of the *S*s and *P*s that adults transform into princess, petite, precious, and prudent. When we're young boys, we're attracted to this feminine ease, but it's a temptation we reject in the most violent possible manner: by beating and destroying, if necessary, but certainly by tormenting with the name we give to the crime: faggot.

Weakness has a skill near to beauty: that of attraction. The attraction of admiration and rage, those two irresistible stirrings. An entrepreneur feels himself attracted by the beauty of a tropical beach and destroys its charm with a big hotel. It's a rape. We rape only what we find beautiful and weak. Strong and beautiful is a physical impossibility, plausible only in porn and maybe in fiction. But what about ugly weakness? The question is whether it's weakness that exerts attraction. And what type of attraction are we talking about? That of destruction. Because it's not just about taking possession or demonstrating dominance—it's that, too, but in the end we dominate something that no longer exists: we want every trace of it gone.

I think about groups of kids at the school and the inevitable fat kid they beat up on, about beggars burned with gasoline in the dead of night, about my sadistic dreams. At school and in the dead of night, there's a mass mentality, group psychology and so on. We beat and burn to feel like part of a group. But it's not just that. I'm thinking of the pleasure of screaming "son of a bitch!" five, ten times in a row from the stands, cursing out the tiny ref way down on the field (who really is a son of bitch), in unison with thousands of others. I think of the cowardice of the individual in a group, and of the great beauty of a group. I think of the chorus of children's voices and my pleasure in patrolling the halls to watch students in each of the classrooms. But I refer as well to one specific instance—*shut up, faggot*—the pleasure of the man who beat me and administered the shocks. Along with the pain came an immense shame: I had known that pleasure.

Of course there's a calculated utility to violence. In today's column, João Ubaldo tells a story about a colonel who orders a peasant to flog some poor soul—another in his command, who'd been coming around to see his daughter—and promises him five hundred bucks to do the deed. The peasant says okay, he'll see to it, but then he comes back saying he'll need help. He returns with his head down, telling the colonel he'll still do what he wants, but he's hesitant. What is it, the cornel asks. *Excuse me, Colonel. If you command it, sir, then I'll do it, but there's no way that man can withstand a lashing worth 500 bucks.* Of course, there's the primary, generic utility of demonstrating power, of showing who's boss, and the specific utilities of vigilante justice, extracting a confession, forcing a victim to flee, smashing the head of the child: by that point it's no longer about good, and heading toward evil. In the schools where I've worked, I've had numerous conversations with parents who hit their children. "Yes sir," they'd say to me, "I know, I already spoke to my wife about it, I was never taught to beat my kids, and I'm not about to start now. I just do what's natural." The first time I heard that phrase, its significance didn't register. How is it they were "never taught to beat" and yet the child's nearly disfigured? Later I realized I'd made an error of calculation. The father only knew how to mete out a five-hundred-dollar beating: he lacked didactic skill with a lash. Beating makes up part of an education and is accepted by children. Ramiro, a nine-year-old boy, told me that when his father got nervous, he would turn red and tremble and punch the walls and break the windows in their house and destroy the furniture. That his father often grabbed his kids and hugged them to his chest, that his grandfather was very violent and his father had promised he'd never beat his own children. But not the mother, who struck them with a rod whenever they did anything wrong. I made a remark, somehow disapproving of the mother. She could barely speak to me, she was so enraged—just look at what the boy's grandfather did to his father. But hitting a kid isn't wrong, Ramiro shot back, it's in the Bible. Jesus hit people who did bad things, and my mother isn't violent, she only hits us when we do something wrong and dad ends up ruining everything in the house.

Who knows. Maybe for José it would have been less humiliating to get his hide tanned from time to time than it was to suffer our father's silence. Who knows. The teachers shamed the parents in their meetings, they call them sir and ma'am and speak softly, almost sweetly, ma'am, your boy is coming to school dirty, you need to teach him to brush his teeth, blow his nose; ma'am, he doesn't do his homework, you need to help us out; sir, he never sits still in class, he's a mess, he can't pay attention to anything, education begins at home;

ma'am, your boy sleeps through class, is he going to bed late? he's cutting class, does he have to be at home to take care of his younger brother? no, he can't, children aren't supposed to work; he's belligerent, has a foul mouth, be careful what you say in front of your children. They name the offspring of malfeasants. And then at home the rod is brandished with lust, the lash comes down and is raised again. The content of these admonitions isn't relevant: they're about shame and public humiliation. Perhaps?

I remember Cecília's shock at the violence she saw in the schools, in the students' families. What can I say? I always knew what to do when one of them came at me. Stare them down, talk it out, listen, strip them of this habit of yelling and beating, otherwise you add to it. Consider the words, hesitations, and expressions of the father, the son, the mother, and try to understand the unique and personal holy spirit which illuminates the triad. Not that I always succeeded. Many times my holy spirit went head to head with that of the family, canceling my ability to listen and see, and I reacted aggressively to the indignation I'd already developed before I even learned the names and life conditions of that mother, that father, that aunt (or neighbor or stepfather or grandmother) who took an eleven-year-old girl into filthy bars to pimp her out, who encouraged their eldest son to whip his sister because she looked the wrong way at the wrong boy. I reacted without knowing that the teacher who spoke with such slow and carefully correct Portuguese had divided the class into blacks and browns and dusky in-betweens, had already identified the snot-nosed kids with skinned knees, unworthy of her precious time. People do what they have to do. What else can I say?

I figure things out by writing them down. The solitude

of my annotations, my authors, and my personal vocabulary helps to organize my reasoning. I'm not writing about my ideas or my work, but about ideas and works. The same goes for public debates, interviews for newspapers and magazines: there's a specific battle being waged, a real point in play, and my voice makes an intervention in what I know. But memory? I manage to understand the posterity of ideas, because they're a single development, albeit fraught and divided, of what came before, and an argument over what will come next, and next, and next.

> *A lone rooster does not a morning make:*
> *he will always need the other roosters.*
> *One to gather up this cry of his*
> *and send it out with another; and another rooster*
> *to gather up the cry of the cock before*
> *and send it out with another, and the other roosters*
> *who along with many other cocks crisscross*
> *the morning sunbeams with their crows*
> *Thus the morning, from its first tenuous thread*
> *is woven among all the roosters.*
> [...]

João Cabral de Melo Neto—*"Weaving the Morning,"* 1962–65

The word, like movement, is divine, without any conjugation, not even the impersonal third person, without tense except the present. It is what is offered. Appearing and appearance. A tenuous thread—this we understand quite well, I suppose— that one sends out and another gathers up, and the morning is made by the crossing of various threads being woven. We understand that many different songs make up the morning. The song is made in the singing. And not just one song: many are necessary. Okay, okay. And now they're songs, attention, that's plural, not the singular with "songs," nor with "roosters." Okay, okay. Calm down, don't get ahead of yourself. It's easy, concordance, it seems obvious, very well, but you won't get the point just by saying okay. Try to say no sometimes. Say, no, one rooster certainly can make something. *He* makes: this is important, too. The rooster is important, not only his song. His solitary song is still a song and from it springs the light. And the fact that he sings it is important, even if his song never echoes. You understand this option for saying no? Let's get a little further into yes. Pay attention, Lígia, we're moving on, don't accept things so quickly, resist a little, savor the taste, find it strange. Or, okay, let's devour it, absorb it with enchantment, let it touch all of our senses, just read it and swallow. Yes, that's it, your disposition toward the world, the whole world, which goes on forming itself in a sequence of yesses. And one day, maybe today, you'll sing and in your song everything you've swallowed will resound. The song that Marta's generation will hear and weave into other mornings. I leave Lígia to the side: she learned how to swallow me with various nos and estrangements. She sings her own song now. It seems I only know how to think adversarially. That's what's lacking in this interview—not merely the feeling of the verb in the past tense, this interest in the solitary cock crow, not so much his song as his person—but not knowing with whom I argue.

Protagonist, antagonist, agony and agora. Each comes from a single word in Greek, that game of men: speaking in public, jousting, leading, driving, attracting, building, making, passing the time, carrying, dragging, driving, pulling, evaluating, educating, litigation, prosecution, mortal anguish. I think in terms of dictionary entries and dictionary entries are a dead language; modern Greek is Greek to me. Another characteristic of my reasoning: I need a process, I dig to the root. But the root only tells what trace remains in current speech. Diachrony and synchrony don't mix. Diachrony explains the process until now, the journey through the uses a word has served. Synchrony explains the push and pull of other words that now exist. A word is only worth its relation to other words in use at a given time. The process up to now, the word's past struggles—none of that counts. I'd already picked up the vice of diachrony by the time I married Eliana, and with her it got even worse. Strange, I wasn't an intellectual until I knew her, in the more-than-biblical sense, or in the precise biblical sense, but without the lewd connotation that the phrase has today. Just look! How can I go on without due consideration of each word? Times like these I envy Dona Joana's chattering mouth. Even her written words. Look what a difference it makes: Dona Joana and D. Joana. To the ear it's the same thing, it refers to the same person. But one form, Dona Joana, puts forward a common, friendly face, while D. Joana reminds us of social hierarchies and the vestiges of an ancient nobility. Madame, my lady, Elaine, that's what I called her, more of a heteronym than a nickname.

Eliana is solar, open to the world, four clearly demarcated syllables. It demands her place. Elena is close, intimate, three syllables, the first an folksy introduction, almost a greeting, my friend, the next one languid, hanging like bunting, and the third like the mumble of a girl, my girl, my mother. Elena wasn't Armando's sister, she was my wife. She almost wasn't Lígia's mother, my wife. Elena and Eliana both visit me. Eliana was the wordsmith, who insisted on etymologies and origins, the one I was thinking of just now. But Elena is the one I miss the most. Mine. Eliana thinks and writes here with me: she works and argues. She clears the way for me and reveals my tantrums as folly. Or she makes them serious by stripping away my shrill anger, and with those sparks and conflagrations she tends a fertile and everlasting flame. Eliana is conscientious and cannot tell a lie. She likes to think calmly, she knows how to fight like no one else because with her what's right is right and what's wrong is wrong—and she's always in the right. Elena is sly and skittish, she lies like child who is hungry, afraid, or lazy. She desperately needs me, she feels cold at night, she needs to entwine her legs with mine, rest her head on my chest and speak softly about her fears. She loves when I bring home a treat and sulks when I forget. Marizpan is her favorite.

I hear Eliana clearly. In bed at night, it doesn't scare me when her voice calls to me. I don't hear Elena: what visits me is the absence of her legs and the weight of her head on my chest. I couldn't hold her tight over the telephone, and that was what she needed. There was an intense struggle in her voice, on that public telephone in Paris. Fearful Elena alternated with upright Eliana, and this was something I found strange, even frightening. My God, it's so sad. I couldn't embrace her, she couldn't see my eyes, her hands had gone cold around the receiver. This impossibility will never leave me. Nor the frozen, stabbing pain that blooms in my chest and snaps my bones every time I remember her voice, her chill, and the distance that separated our bodies. What didn't she know, Luiza?—tell me, goddammit, what was it she never knew? I didn't kill Armando. Eliana, I didn't talk, can you hear me, my little one, my darling girl, I didn't talk. But at the time I didn't know this hypothesis hovered over her. How could I?

I didn't talk, and it's just though I did. I know this, I know that you understood this right away. My Eliana, so sincere. If you were to lay your head on my chest, that chancre would always be there, you thought—growing, occupying the space reserved for our affection. It's still here, my love, pulsing and aching, and I can no longer smell your hair, or feel the drool that ran from your mouth in allergy season.

And now I'm going to talk with that girl Cecília, who never met you. She sent me a message commenting on my reports. She's intelligent and inquisitive, she liked my writing, she wants to make an appointment to interview me next week, here at the house. A lot of people never met you, Eliana. My wife, with her serious gestures and delayed laugh. Codename Joyce, vulgar in every sense, he says he fucked you, my love. I'm talking nonsense and I can't even manage to get angry anymore when I remember the meetings you organized around him with your psychologist friends. Today, Codename Joyce is a middlebrow writer, respected by new young women he'll claim to have fucked. But my anger has passed. Secret meetings, sex was undergoing a revolution, too, mine and yours, Eliana. Who was the bastard who gave you that glow? No one, I swear, there was no one. No one, I assure myself, it was no one. Thin, tall, bony, and ugly. He has a Southern accent, he knows things about history, books, and people. A storyteller. He loved telling stories about what would happen next: a new world, new men and women. His thinness, his accent, his undercover ways, it all went together, corroborating his girlish, prophetic speech. A filter for the New Age, the honest old scheme erased from the eternal macho desire of sheltering and consuming. The strained juices of the new truths had tasted bitter. For Armando I kept quiet, I fed and sheltered him, for how long, Eliana? Three weeks? Two months?

My wife worked in the university clinic. She'd just obtained a position in a research hospital and was preparing for the admission exams to get her master's degree. After defending my thesis in pedagogy, I'd decided once and for all to go into education and had recently managed to be made the principal of a group of schools far from home. We worked a lot, both of us beneath the wing of a state that became more claustrophobic every day. We were mobilized, taking people in, hiding guns, debating what kind of revolution it would be. On the other hand, we lived among lunatics and children, something I now realize afforded us a view of the world where dictatorship and revolution weren't as deterministic as they were in our friends' hearts.

In Portuguese, the verb denotes both time and person. In what other language can you respond only with a conjugated verb? Are you going to Maria's house? *Vou.* Wanna eat? *Quero.* Do you like eggplant? *Odeio.* We barely ever say yes. I happen to use it quite often, the crisp yes or no. It was a choice that became a habit, and after I say it, I frighten myself. Are you going to Maria's house? Yes. Do you like Codename J.? No. I realize that it's considered rude, appears rude, because it is. It doesn't continue the sequence of movement begun by the question: it interrupts it and has nothing to add. It borders on confrontation. I don't really know why I do it. I remember that at the beginning, as a young adult, I liked the cutting effect, the unaccustomed word that surprises: it was for fun, for the experience of a new word rolling in my mouth. Yes. No. Maybe it had something to do with the objectivity of scientific language, which then I understood, and a certain rude revolutionary tone that I was picking up. Revolution and science both vanished but the yes and the no remained, became habitual. (A cop responds, affirmative, the soccer player, definitely.) "To gather up this cry of his" and "the cry of a cock before"—the absence of the verb obscures the person and the tense, it leaves us in suspense. But, strangely, it maintains the idea of movement, perhaps reinforces it. The speech of children, of parents with children, and of the insane: all contain this reinforcement of absence. The notes that old Joaquim jotted down knew something of this force, but José's memoirs do not. Science, its language, understands it, and for this reason avoids it. I learned to write the book of nature, the absences contained by the exuberant real must be filled out in a way that distills it to words intelligible to everyone along the chain of knowledge.

This is what I thought about as they beat me. What language would be safer: the babble of the *homo demens* or the precision of *homo sapiens*—which would hide more? And safer for whom? Was protecting Armando the same as protecting Lígia and Marta? Eliana and Lígia? I had to tell a viable story even though I'd lost control of my speech. They didn't let us sleep, and I knew that stress and fatigue were going to undermine my intelligence. For this reason the story had to be linked to something profoundly true. A piece of me that could stand on its own, coherent when all other strength had deserted me, when my body was no longer mine. They were experts in thrashing, the bastards; my colleagues in confession by installment. I had nothing, was stupid tired, blind as an illiterate. Codename Joyce was out of the country, safe and sound, so I could concentrate on talking about him. I never knew how the other five or six who had passed through the house ended up, so I had to keep quiet about them. And Armando, where was he? And Eliana? I didn't know anything. Was one of her friends part of the organization? And of my friends: who was, and who wasn't? I didn't know anything, so I couldn't say much. Everyone was very professional, they went to the movies, had beers together, even discussed politics, and any one of them could have spearheaded a kidnapping, or driven a getaway car for a bank robbery. Even Eliana: how far had she gone? I wasn't even sure about my own father: which side was he on? In this story, I was the only fool.

José, in his book, describes a boy with various small joys, the morning of manhood, joys as a youth, youthful joys. Powerful things—the intensity of desire and its fulfillment; shamelessness, with its low manners with filthy words; delight. There was a time when everything was morning and he captured it.

> Our mother left the room. I was old enough to go to school with my brothers, and Amado called to me from his bed. "What is it?" I asked—I didn't want to be late for breakfast. The smell of coconut soap and G.'s neatly made bed, the powerful, indolent mess of Amado: I was between the two, wanting my mother.
> —Come look at this.
> And he threw his covers off, between the beds, and showed me the little tent he was able to make with his erection.
> —Look, can you do this?
>
> José—*unpublished manuscript*

And Amado helps José do as he did. The description and the details are cheerful and childish, their slang naturalizing the sex—at first.

> The Velhas River baths, deep in the country, in shadows, light skins under clothing, the dark skin of the jabuticaba. Deep in the country, so much foliage, the smell of the forest, dicks out. Vianinha's was absurd, he was already fully grown, he had pubic hair and was spurting a drip of sperm. Nobody wanted anything to do with him, for fear of losing the milky way. With

the younger ones he didn't do any harm, it was just a matter of pressing into the gully and never going in. Just for laughs. He was the big guy and got pissed whenever he found himself rejected. He went around the rowdy and ready semicircle playfully tugging on all their pricks. Everything made us laugh in that dawn of our lives, in that beloved childhood that the times don't allow anymore. Everything made us laugh at that age when sex is funny and hadn't yet become the pungent drama that it became in the afterlives of a boy: life as an adult, masculine strength, maturity, old age—not even the louche, nauseating, hedonistic leering of dirty old men.

Pedro Nava—*O círio perfeito*, 1983

In our neighborhood there were also thick groves of jabuticaba, light and dark flesh, and José proceeds now to an urbane and exhibitionist language that makes me want to jump out of my skin. What sort of amalgam of people is this Amado? I'm outraged by that scene in our room, and afraid of what will come.

In prison my rage derived from my own stupidity. I wasn't mad because I was stupid, but because I'd been stupid, I hadn't foreseen, I hadn't prepared myself. I didn't perceive the soldiers as adversaries, but as enemies, and that made all the difference. We inhabited different universes, without communication or common origins. There were no points of contact, only points of friction. It sounds crazy, incoherent, illogical, inexcusable for a scientist—but this was how I saw things and it was why I wasn't prepared. Armando adopted the same logic as the soldiers: he accepted the idea that we were at war. How did he fall? Some unsuspected person had betrayed him. Nobody needed to betray me or Eliana, we were just collateral damage.

Unsuspected because think about it: he believed he was at war, he plotted things out carefully and took precautions, he only gave up names of those he believed couldn't hurt the cause (me and her). I knew nothing about Armando's life as a militant, and for that reason was a harmless choice. When I found out, later, I understood it—I was going to say his guerilla street smarts, his power as a strategist—anyway, I admire those who are capable of engagement to the limit, who can go all the way to death for the cause, and who do it with intelligence and clarity. In fact, I envy anyone capable of this level of enchantment, and above all I admire their intelligence. Even during the busiest months of his involvement in the movement, he still visited us often. We ate together, went to the movies. Then he'd disappear for a few days or weeks. He came back happy. We doubted he was involved in anything dangerous, that he was part of a militant cell, but we endeavored not to know much. In any case, Armando denied it—he said they were meetings for political debates, that yes, he could be imprisoned because in those days almost anyone could be thrown in jail. He said he helped organize the resistance, aided his comrades, but he rejected the armed struggle because it risked the entire democratic organization that was forming, that with guns we'd lose the solidarity of the bourgeoisie. The guns we hid for him always belonged to some idiot who got himself in a bind—and Armando couldn't let them walk around armed, so he gave them to us for a few days' safekeeping. If a friend of ours disappeared, he never knew more than the same rumors we heard. All this is to say that we intuited, but never knew for certain, that he was one higher ups in the armed struggle. Our ignorance protected him, and the banal social life with his sister and his brother-in-law was a useful ruse.

A bitter gag and tang shuts my throat, my esophagus burns. Armando exposed us to danger. And I let him, I knew the times we were living in, and the consequences of what he was doing. But how could I refuse to help him? Exactly that: how could I refuse to help in those times we were living in? We were compromised. There were rumors. There were. Listen. The banks of the Ipiranga were listening. Who listens to rumors beyond the banks of the Ipiranga? Rumors and humors: there must be some relation. One is sonorous and the other is liquid. What they have in common is the way they spread. Rumors are intelligible and apprehensive words in any language and culture, which even the mute can murmur and the deaf can hear, betrayal is betrayal wherever you go, like fucking the woman whose husband is saving your ass. The rumor of a train, river, stampede, surrender. It rumbles through the air, enters the body through various channels of audition, the way the beat of a drum first enters through the abdomen, the genitals. The rumblings aren't understood—they're incorporated. They take shape without cognition. We know that someone has betrayed. Or fucked. Or surrendered. It's known. It's said. It's reported. The subject isn't just indefinite, it's inexistent. The same as the subject of "it rained yesterday." What rained? There is no subject. Who talked? Who said? Inexistent, and therefore unassailable, the victim defenseless.

If it were possible. My story perceived as a rumbling, without words, without voice, but incorporated whole, solid. In fact, that's how things are. Our image of the world is the sum of various rumors, reverberations of the steps we do and do not take passing through us. There is no alibi, no way to repair the story that we end up with. José, with his book, expands my childhood laterally, into things I never knew. Because my house and my family are me, in a sense. I was the the eldest brother—I thought I managed it. When Agnello slapped José in the face, I felt it on my skin. When Armando was condescending to my father, the matter rested with me. It was the same at school: when a teacher called a student a monkey, I was the humiliated black boy *and* the racist teacher. What amalgamations are these? We need to be thoroughly adapted to a given habitat, but if we're becoming part of that habitat at the same time, what results? Who's creating the placenta, the uterus, the fetus? It seems as if each of us goes about constructing our own environment with the available elements, whatever's at arm's length, outside the self. And the environments intersect and coincide and occupy the same space: my house and José's house. I am an element in José's environment and vice versa. The same goes for Armando. And suddenly a rupture: José with his book for example, ruptures the history of my room, and ruptures my story, the story of my family, just think: something about back then has now changed. Everything else will have to adapt and be reshaped.

This interview, Cecília, the letter reports, the interrogations, my nonconfessions: what are they? Why do I mix these diverse people and moments? Having nothing to do is making me crazy. The responsibility that words possess, says Helena the teacher. My torturers took pleasure in beating, but they didn't beat anybody up just for pleasure. They did it to collect information. There was no didactic motive, nothing punitive or vengeful, it was only part of their investigative work, collecting information to fill in the bigger picture of the organized resistance. In the end they knew more about the organizations than the organizations knew about themselves. This girl is aiming for the same thing. After these interviews she'll know more about the period than the people who lived through it. But, as under torture, they each will tell her only what doesn't threaten, what doesn't weigh on their present. And so, perhaps it's not possible to have a collective return to what happened, only an individual one. The interviews will give her just the external elements within arm's length, the shared elements from which each individual constructs his shell, his placenta. And from within herself, the girl who never lived through it will have to draw out another witness, old enough to be convincing, an artifice that enchants.

But she says she read what I wrote. I haven't left behind only rumors. Hardly. I take responsibility for what I've written and done, for the fights I fought: I am also this history, and I rather like the old man who's emerging from it, I feel like I could touch him. Even when I hear one of my lines being butchered or distorted in the mouth of a student, another professor, or an ill-intentioned adversary, I still recognize myself, esteem my words. What I've left is strong and hard. In the professional development courses I helped organized and teach, I went back to having daily contact with the schools. For fifteen years I'd remained distant, just an evaluation here and there. And they were always office conversations with coordinators, secretaries, ministers, advisers—never this direct contact with the teachers. I honestly don't know if the teachers got anything out of the courses, but it was certainly productive for the university faculty who taught them. An opportunity for discovering new ideas, some of them brilliantly simple, devised by teachers who were brimming over with talent: an interface between those who teach how to teach and those who teach how to learn. I don't know how many times these interfaces ever led to a transformation in the way things are done, I don't know how many of us discerned the richness of opportunity raised by the teachers' boredom and bad attitudes—their repressed rage against the

State, the students, and the parents; against us, academia, and the country—against life.

In the final analysis, a school is a representation of the world that excludes us, the teachers: school is preparation for a life that teachers don't have. School was my refuge for many years. There I knew things, and the world could be drawn with lines that gave it a unity and precise contours. My sanity and survival require, more than air, to draw these boundaries around that which is dispersed: to teach the limits, the categories, the phyla, the families, the species; to contain the unbearable confusion of life in elements that were comprehensible in my state of abandonment. Teaching science to fifth graders saved me from the chaos. They were still well nourished students, those kids in the Seventies. They resembled the boy I'd been. The teacher's power, in the public schools, remained untouched. It came from us, the teachers, that questioning of hierarchies, the provocations designed to unsettle the students, transform them into inquiring beings, in possession of doubts and desires. The oppression that quieted us during teachers' meetings and in the occasional contact we had with the various organs of the Department of Education, or when dealing with agents of public order who would go to high schools, apartment complexes, and clubs in search of subversives (to public order), and even at the tables of the bars I no longer visited: that oppression vanished in the classroom. In my science classes. To the state I was a principal and to the city I was a teacher. At night I taught adult education, and in the morning I graded papers, I finished all the paperwork for my district. In my work I hid the sad and troublesome monster who had developed in me. Battered, traitor, killer, widower, father, and orphan.

Armando was given up for my sake, but not by my lips,

as though that made any difference. My imprisonment must have forced him to expose himself: he had to arrange for Eliana's flight, mobilize people to come visit me, and make my imprisonment known. He had to take to the battlefield.

I was lucky that my family immediately learned I'd been taken prisoner. I was supposed to meet my father and didn't turn up. So my father figured out what had happened. Even people who weren't caught up in the resistance had rendezvous points. There were places. Anything could happen. We stayed connected. It was lucky because when the family figures out where the missing person is, the cops are leery of snuffing him out, you know? Because if he's found dead after being arrested, then it's obvious who did it. So they always tried to avoid that kind of thing. It's like I was telling you.... I was found almost immediately. Even the torture I went through: I get the impression that it wasn't as bad as it could have been, given what I learned later. About houses rented by the police for the purpose of summary executions. They'd take their most wanted prisoners there and no one would ever know what happened. They had a whole security system set up and everything, and they'd kill them after the interrogations. They killed them when they were finished them: that's how they made people disappear. But at the time I didn't know these houses existed.

Someone like me—*recent conversation*

I was probably taken prisoner because of him. In cases like these we all forgot the visible, incontestable cause: the men who had come to my house and took me, the men who went to his hideout and killed him. Soldiers, the secret police, Operation Bandeirantes, the prisons of constituted power. They weren't the cause of betrayals and deaths, of humiliations and sufferings, of suicides and madness, because they were enemies: that was their role. Even I, who had never positioned myself as anyone's enemy, thought of them that way. I searched for causes in the guts, in mine and those of my friend, in the meanderings of a movement whose logic I didn't understand.

—*Josélia lashed out a lot, she was a real a violent kid. And I hit back, for real. The neighbors used to say she was going to end up crazy. Some of this remained in her, maybe that's why she's so responsible now. She was always up to something. She wanted to walk along the top of every wall. She never wore pants or shorts, only a dress, and she got up on the walls.*

—*I got a note from the principal saying Dinarte put his hand on some girl's butt. She didn't ask me to come to her office, only sent me the note. When Dinarte came home I asked him, are you perverted or something? And he says, but mom, but mom. And I said, no, just tell me, are you some kind of pervert who puts his hand on people's butts? And he looks at me and says, but I'm a man. Oh, Jesus, why? I slapped him right across the mouth. So you get to touch people just because you're a man? His father grounded him from playing ball for two weeks, which is what he likes more than anything else. So that's how we're dealing with it.*

—*Why should a kid respect his teacher if he doesn't even respect his own mother and father? The parents are to blame. You're right about that. I don't lay a hand on my son, and I guess what you're telling me is that's the problem, he doesn't get smacked enough.*

—*Okay, what you say about the boys beating up on the younger ones, that's definitely true. The principal said that at recess the big boys are beating up the smaller kids, they gang up on them. I told her, let me give you a suggestion: call up all the able-bodied mothers and fathers who are out of work and get them to help keep an eye on things at recess. It was just a suggestion, it's what they did in another school my son went to. It was just a suggestion I had. So I told her. But she said, no, we can't have things mixed up like that. But I see it at home, the boys beating each other up. From my house I can see the whole block, and you know what, they like doing it—beating each other up. They do it for no reason at all. You can see it on their faces: they love it.*

Group of mothers—*recently*

In the Seventies it was never an issue. Not in the Thirties, either. Graciliano Ramos was jailed by the Estado Novo and never said anything about getting beat up. He was thrown in prison, taken out of circulation. When he got out, his comrades in the Communist Party asked him to write a book denouncing the oppressive regime. He ended up writing the *Prison Memoirs* many years later. But right after he got out everybody insisted that he had to make a denunciation right away. What he wrote instead was *Childhood*. The characters were a scrawny boy, his father, his uncles, the teacher, the principal, the priest, the deputy, and his grandfather, all living in the Brazilian scrub. This was the oppressive regime the book was about. He's beaten, but it wasn't the point of the book. Being beaten isn't the subject of any book. But the fear of being beaten, that's huge—the fear of making a mistake, fear of not realizing it, fear of making another mistake, the fear of being afraid. Fear isn't the subject, it's too big. He can't speak. But maybe, to return to the beating, he might get used to it. He does the math to see if any kind of infraction is worth the price he'll pay in brusies, then he goes ahead with it. The greater terror, perhaps, is of the arbitrary, the unexpected.

For me the greatest terror was not knowing when it would stop. Maybe if I'd been beaten as a child … But I wasn't accustomed to it. It's true that you learn quick, and I wasn't old yet, so I learned. But it's only ever partial. What I mean is that there's no way to stop hoping it will end, or that they'll at least have a shred of solidarity and respect. This is a mechanism that undermines resistance and it has to be fought, but you can never do away with it altogether. Hope is a false word; it has a sound and a spelling whose referent is void, like a counterfeit bill, a phantom pregnancy, it transforms from a feeling into an action, from noun into verb. There should be a rule to prevent making transitive verbs into nouns. The nouns are sufficient, and so are the intransitive verbs. Fighting, dying, changing, fleeing are fine as fight, death, change, flight. The student says: but food isn't the same as the act of eating. That's right, food is the object of the verb. And is love the act of loving? No, perhaps love is the verb's subject.

With respect to the case of the word *hope*, I think the complication stems from the definition of hope as a passive desire, of impotent origins and, in instances where the noun is used, unconfessed. Its meaning in the sentence "I hope to give you a two hour lunch break" is the same as "I hope that she still loves me." In the first phrase we can't change the verb to a noun: you can't say, "I have hope that I'll give you a two hour lunch break," but in the second phrase, semantically, it would still be correct to say, "I hold on to the hope that she still loves me," even though I'd never say that. What I mean is that having hope, in this case, is recognizing impotence, the fact that she probably doesn't love me and that keeping hope alive is only a vain foolishness of the spirit. Weakness.

The classic mechanism is not hoping, bracing for impact, and steeling the nerves: it's been twenty-nine years and I still must be ready to withstand. Readiness. It's become a dependence—repeating the meanings of words like a stutterer, harmonizing their spheres of action—or is it sharpening?

It takes all the strength of my spirit to transform my executioners into animals, not to leave the slightest opening, to discuss nothing, not even Pelé. Which is impossible, I never met anyone who couldn't. And that is how along with fear, shame takes its hold. Because it's ugly. The pleasure in the beatings—the men's faces, the blood, the blows, the laughter, a theater, vomit, that swaying light, the fatigue of the men doing the beating, their sweat, the white belly that appears under the rumpled blue shirt, the nose studded with blackheads, my groans, their crooked teeth, my acting, not withstanding, the fear of dying, crying, and trying not to register what I saw, not understand what I was looking at, forget. We were all men, and it's impossible to erase the information from my neurons. We were men.

> The first Russian patrol came in view of the camp around midday on January 27, 1945.... They didn't greet us, didn't smile; they appeared oppressed, not only by pity but by a confused restraint, which sealed their mouths, and riveted their eyes to the mournful scene. It was a shame well-known to us, the shame that inundated us after the selections and every time we had to witness or submit to an outrage: the shame that the Germans didn't know, and which the just man feels before a sin committed by another. It troubles him that it exists, that it has been irrevocably introduced into the world of things that exist, and that his goodwill availed nothing, or little, and was powerless to defend against it.
>
> So for us even the hour of freedom struck solemn and oppressive, and filled our hearts with both joy and a painful sense of shame, because of which we would have liked to wash from our

consciences and our memories the monstrosity that lay there;
and with anguish, because we felt that this could not happen,
that nothing could ever happen that was good and pure enough
to wipe out our past, and that the marks of the offense would
remain in us forever, and in the memories of those who were
present, and in the places where it happened, and in the stories
that we would make of it.

Primo Levi—*The Truce*, 1963

We let it happen, we occasioned this horror. And we continue to occasion, it happens, we are still men.

My mother brought cornbread and guava jam to the jailers, and to us, the prisoners. My father only came a few times, wanting to know what the men had asked me. He said, hold out just a little longer, we'll get you out, you'll be out soon.

There, like now, I was the odd one. I was thirty years old and the other guys were only eighteen, twenty, sixteen. There was a lot going on, a lot had happened and it formed a part of those kids' flesh. They told me about festivals, sang songs, had long hair. I'd seen the festivals and I knew the songs, my hair wasn't cut short. How can I explain? I'd heard Joyce Moreno, her cultural proselytizing, but I hadn't realized there could be any truth in it. Music, hair, clothes, sex as a form of ideology and not of culture. That was strange, captivating, powerful, exclusive. I didn't understand. Because ideological proselytizing was something I understood and either combatted or adhered to. What I mean is it was familiar to me. I argued with Armando, who was cynical enough to be sensible about those kinds of things. But through his jesting I discerned not only a rigidity of ideas, but a discipline of action I warded off in myself: I feared the absence of fear and the feeling of the infinite.

I was a militant communist. I joined the Party when I saw Moscow holding off the German tanks. I got the impression that it justified, after the fact, everything I thought it was impossible to admit about Stalinist Communism, a kind of hardness necessary for resistance, for winning the war. […]

I lived in a feeling of the infinite, like anyone who was a communist.

Edgar Morin—*No One Knows What Day It Will Be Born*, 1992

I'm inverting everything. What used to drive me away from my friends is now something I need. A totalizing vision throwing open the doors of the world, the whole world, its entire history, the primates, us, everywhere, yes, because this explanation is powerful and was something that could open access to every last corner, even to our souls and the hereafter. I understood that everything was coated in authoritarian ignorance, willingly, everyone was amputating their sensibility to reality, exempting ourselves from the efforts of the struggle. We mutilated our sensory capabilities and subjective intelligence when we enslaved ourselves to the notion of analysis. Right out of the gate, the war was lost.

But now, retired and cynical, I perceive—in Cecília, in Helena the teacher, in my conversations with Lígia, in the interviews I did with teachers, principals, and students; in the schools and the university and the world—the disservice that turning a blind eye does us. I used to be profoundly irritated by the truisms of Sérgio Buarque de Holanda, with his lazy, proud, and egotistical Lusitanians, his indolent and predatory Indians, and his disgust for what it all said about us. But today I see these as characters that allowed him to construct powerful instruments of observation and analysis.

His idea was confident, but deceptive, I thought then, and illusive. But it gave him the power and the will to build a world, to wade into the past, to seize the future and take from it those visions that moved us.

It's necessary to have a point of view and a question. And my friends had them, which irritated me. I don't know if it was the fault of biology in general, and its strict sense of scientific investigation, or of genetics specifically—the paternal side. Instruments of observation that transform the thing observed. Microscope, slide, the muscle of a living, opened frog, research on cadavers, formaldehyde, the mere mention of an illness allows me to smell it and hear it.

> *My strained senses for surprising Malady in the act were constantly improving. My powers of gazing, seeing. Of listening, hearing. Of touching, guessing. To be skilled with* OBSERVA-TION, *even the nose must achieve a refined discernment between smells. I was able to distinguish a countless number of maladies just by smell. I'm not talking about the stench of living putrefaction that rises from miasma and gangrene and nomas. But the notes that emerge from within the general reek of the infirmary: the odor of violets and vinegar that signal a diabetic coma; the fecal curdling of those infected with typhoid; garlic-scented multijoint rheumatism. So many times a diagnosis only required an exam for formal conformation and to play by the rules of the game. The rules of the game...were not to lose it and not to be deceived by any Malady that hid and remained defiant.*

> Pedro Nava—*Seashore*, 1978

The rules of the game in prison—from which I can't seem to escape, despite there being nothing there that might be useful to me—and this appointment I made, she called to confirm, will be here next week, she and her interview will make me return and I'm imprisoned, there's a weight that makes my thoughts hang back there, thirty-four years ago, like a big cloth sack, full of odds and ends, hiding a misplaced anvil, creating an imbalance that makes it impossible for me to shoulder the sack and keep going without feeling the presence of that anvil the entire time, aware of its exact position and feeling its shape through the sack. The rules of the game in prison were to not die and not give in. The moral structure inverted the order of operations, but instinct screams "don't die, don't die." Francisco Augusto didn't understand how I'd managed to play dumb and take such a beating.

> *You had a convincing story to tell, you weren't a militant, you don't have any idea about what's going on, you don't know anything about any of it. You could say whatever you wanted about Armando, he couldn't have been compromised by what you said. There was nothing you could give away.*

Francisco Augusto—remembrance, 1970

The problem was I didn't know that. I didn't know what a convincing or intelligent story was, I didn't know what it meant to open, to shut, to give way, period. I knew precisely nothing, not even the name of the illness to be sniffed and felt out. Anything could have been a disease, you know? He didn't understand, he thought that I was a borderline masochist for letting myself get so banged up when I had an intelligent story to tell.

> *There's something that's not exactly human, and a little bit diabolic, that allowed you to resist. There's a diabolical side to resistance. Superhuman. It's not human to resist. It's almost a*

pleasure. This heroic side. You entered into a dimension of madness and hallucination, of the heroism of resisting torture.

Francisco Augusto—*remembrance*, 1970

I didn't continue the conversation. I closed my eyes and felt Francisco Augusto resetting my bones, his movements precise, his hot hand securing mine with the necessary pressure, and I didn't feel any pain, only heat and confidence, and my entire muscular system relaxed, slept to the *crack-crack* sound.

The truth was that I stopped thinking about it from any angle; now he returns to obsess me. The very ideal of betrayal that I'd read in the eyes of others, I hadn't read it all the way through. The grumbling of doubt and censure locked into those gazes was merely confirmation of what I carried inside. There is no punishment without blame and I had been punished. And not by gods or by inscrutable destiny, but by my countrymen, my compatriots, my contemporaries.

Aside from blame, I read the pity that, with time, transformed into respect and admiration. I'd made history, I didn't wait for it to happen. Maybe that's why the subject returns now with such force and disturbs me to the point where I can't escape the damned prison where I didn't talk. Sealed into my creed of not believing, only seeing, of keeping my eyes up and spirit alert, the admiration of these young ones disconcerted me. The soldiers weren't Germans, Cecília, and I'm not a Jew, and even if I were, look what monstrosity was born of it, of all that can't be forgotten. Forgiveness doesn't exist, I know, but there has to be a way of living with the terror of what was, without it becoming its inverted semen, historical opposite, Egyptian misfortunes created by a sky god because of the need to have our souls yoked to his. What I didn't say can't be worth more than what I did say later. Having been destroyed made me less: only what I constructed should count. But the youth, the good and the pure, they think that the intensity of rebirth cancels the horror of having died. And that's not true. The cynical and the vain and the vitalists used that new-life eraser to redeem their errors. I understand why João Cabral used to say that his least favorite work was *Morte e vida*. Anyone who reads it forgets the *suffering* and is left with just the life.

The world as oppression doesn't sit well with me. Praising the strong and praising the weak results in the same violent game. When I got back in the classroom I was confused.

> *It was an immense feeling of fear. To give you an idea, when I went home I would get off the bus three or four stops early, I'd try to take different routes home, every night, afraid of being followed, hauled off to jail.*
>
> *The school was visited daily by the secret police because they wanted students, people they thought were our students. So there began to be a series of demands for photographs of everyone at the school, and in other buildings, apartment complexes—it was madness.*

Someone like me—*recently*

There were placards up all over the city, showing photos of terrorists. The newspapers issued warnings to subversive cells, the TV showed which guerrillas had been apprehended. There was a kind of mass schizophrenia in the air, we were all being watched, friends were disappearing, militants and nonmilitants built networks of information to know who was still alive, nothing written or spoken still carried its conventional meaning and the new meanings required deciphering codes that were unstable and for that reason inefficient, the value of face-to-face relations was also placed in suspense:

friend, guerrilla, stool pigeon, colleague, infiltrator, plant—all of them wore jeans, spoke in allegories, used metaphors and code names that swarmed across every available surface—and that idiotic little joy of secret codes, of knowing looks, and the feeling of brotherhood at the dawn of a new day, and also the stubborn, fetid joy of those small men who had the power to denounce, threaten, shout. And besides all that there was the street, the bus, the bakery, the line at the bank, soap operas, lovers, the life of *good morning, how's it going, four rolls, please, a double shot*, people going to work and coming home, the bus jammed, grinding against each other, people laughing and people sleeping, long conversations, stench of armpits, the driver smoking, an old lady saying *excuse me* in her tiny voice, a big black man yelling *you sons of bitches, can't you see the lady wants to get by, bunch of punks*, the day completely normal, words meaning what they mean, every gesture in place, I tighten my grip, wave, and wonder of wonders, *our team in 1970.*

In meetings with teachers and coordinators, in the communications with the district office, in the classroom with my students, I tried to be as clear as possible. I was horrified by the metaphors and by the whispers, I felt then lost the fear that wormed its way into us, and had slowly frozen me in the period before I went to prison. I'd gone mute in the interrogations. I used to talk all the time, and then I only required punctual attendance, objectivity and synthesis, all my lesson plans and reports filled out just like they want, staff meetings and minutes, I knew about all the students and every teacher. I met with parents afflicted by the changes taking place in their children and in the times we lived in, and told them to stick by their kids. I managed to open the school at night and created an adult education program, a lot of the parents came, the teachers were all volunteers. I'd made inquiries with the comptroller and the cops who came after our staff wanting to know about the classes in civic and moral education, social organization, and Brazilian politics. *What do you want to know, sir? Here are the syllabi, the summary of material we taught in each class, attendance, absences, tests, evaluations. The tone of the classes? The students' comments? Well, sir, in the event that our reports aren't sufficiently clear, I invite you to sit in on some of our classes.* Sometimes they were confused by the materials I gave them, for example on Greek democracy. I summoned the social studies teacher and asked him if he would please be so kind as to offer a private session of his class for these gentlemen. The cops got annoyed and left in a huff. In my classes and in meetings, whenever anyone raised an issue that flirted with danger, began speaking in code, or made any wisecrack about the soldiers I interrupted, furious: "Hey, I'm a spy, didn't you know? I could be, so watch it." I called any student or teacher who missed class, or I sent someone to check on them at home. Not everybody had phones. If someone disappeared, we had to be quick.

> So then we talked to the lawyers and they said, "look, you have to make them see that people know about this prison, that the public is aware, and maybe then they'll relax"—something like that. We scheduled a meeting. "Whoever is single"—me and two others—"should go talk to them." So we went, marched right up to the door of the secret police: "We want to speak to the director here." "Why?" "He has to sign some checks, and tomorrow we have to run payroll"—something like that. I remember that it was a hot day, very hot, and the guard was fat and sweating, sweating, sweating and we just went right up and started talking to him. His team was Santos, we got him talk-

ing about Pelé, who knows what else, and he ended up work-ing it out. Of course that wasn't why he was released, but ... I sometimes get to thinking about how crazy it all was, heading straight for the gates of ... My God, my God.

Someone like me—*recent conversation*

In the adult education classes the suffocation was even greater. It attracted insanity from both sides. Educating adults was necessarily subversive: this was pretty much the consensus of anyone in power—those who thought that teaching people to read and write was suspect—as well as the radical teach-ers whose sole objective, the one that gave legitimacy to any action, including making love, was to topple the repressive powers and herald the inevitable triumph of socialism. Some of our high-school students were tutors at night school. Along with Lucilia, I organized the program, and taught science and Portuguese. She was already a university professor and couldn't help out every night, so she would write up the les-sons plans for Portuguese and I'd teach a double. The other teachers were younger, right out of college or still finishing up. The most circumspect were the ones most deeply involved in the heavier stuff. I feared for their safety, but their ears and eyes were closed with the wax seal of revolution. Some were wonderful people: serious, generous, and good teachers. Many of them died. They were just a little younger, but I felt like a grandfather to them, in various senses. Including, some-thing I'd never thought about, in terms of sex.

I'd lost lust, like the eunuch minister at court, I only had the desire to make, organize, teach, work, direct, make sure everything was going okay and that nobody was getting hurt, challenge, and provoke. I had a gentle nostalgia, not for sex, but for desire. I didn't even feel the urge and I didn't even think about it, if a double *didn't even* makes any sense: I appreciated catching the long looks the young teachers would give a colleague when she turned to walk away, or blush as she got closer, or the stammering of a young teacher when one of her comrades slipped into her class. There was also the flouncing of bodies, the laughter that ended with a head on a friend's shoulder, a tête-à-tête in which the boy clasps the girl's arm to hold her attention, to place more emphasis on his words, to feel the smoothness of her skin, to which she responds by lowering her eyes, raising them up again with unconvincing coyness. Little things like that moved me in the same way as Lígia's first attempts at words took hold of me. I saw an extraordinary power in these beginnings, like when my students discover the meaning of one of João Cabral's poems, which minutes before had been an unintelligible foreign language. The throat tightens. I had, in those days, a claustrophobic feeling of love and compassion for the world, in which I included myself. We were small and weak and there was no way out, and at the same time we were together, united not in the struggle or for the cause or anything like that, but in life. It was that simple. Hence the apparent schizophrenia and lucid paranoia, on the one hand, and the bus, the bakery, the national soccer team on the other—none of it stayed my hand, they didn't appear under the sign of antagonism, there was still some life in common.

And life, for me, at that time, translated only as work and Lígia. I'm talking about '71, maybe '72, a year after Eliana and Armando died, a year after my father's illness. Not the national team of 1970, but months later. I think I left prison in March and the World Cup was in June. My father had had his first stroke in May, something like that, just before the Cup.

When I got out of prison he was there to receive me. Prickly and firm, quiet as always, but with something else I didn't recognize. A sadness lurked in his daily routine. He took me by the arm, touched my face with hands I don't remember having felt before, confirming something but not seeming to see me. It wasn't me he was looking for, that was the feeling I got. Jussara says that I looked awful when I got home: skinny, bearded, bruised, and scowling like an angry animal. She and my mother both looked at me differently: swift glances from the corner of their eyes to make certain it was still me inside that disjointed man. But this period of estrangement finally passed. Women have that way of bathing, feeding, making the bed, fluffing the pillow; they bleed, become pregnant, have many bodies and many ways of doing their hair, painting their nails—what I mean is that their bodies are always a field of change and manipulation. They cry more often, too— more things enter and leave them. After we passed through the phase of feeling things out they welcomed me with care, and things slowly returned to normal between us. But not with my father. Something in him had broken.

We were all sad about Armando's death. We didn't talk much about it. When Eliana died next it was an earthquake. Mother, Jussara, and I steadied ourselves in the doorframes to keep from collapsing, to prevent the earth from swallowing us whole. Not my father: perhaps by then he'd died. Or maybe he'd already said his goodbyes to Eliana. I don't know when. When I got out of prison, he touched me, he really held me by the arm, firmly, but there was no tenderness in his face. He ran his fingers across my mouth and eyes, like a blind man might do. He looked deep into my eyes and then abruptly turned to leave. We got to talk a bit before his second stroke, when he became completely mute.

When I got involved in the student movement in '59 or '60, writing for the student newspaper and making handouts for my test prep classes, my father helped me with my writing. In a still more distant past, when he still played with Armando, in those moments when he taught Armando his music, I was embarrassed. He must have been about forty-something and we were twelve or thirteen. At the time, my father seemed to me a complete and finished being. Even when he practiced and took on that dreamlike air, or when he laughed with his friends and played his silly games at the table while he had his cigarette, coffee and bread—making little creatures from a hunk of bread and then devouring them cannibalistically, tearing limb from limb—none of this broke the fourth wall. He was a great man despite his weak body and his spells of self-absorption, his intrinsic pessimism, and his failure to become a musician. The joy he took when he played with Armando didn't derive from friendly showboating—his concentration wasn't the same as when he practiced alone. Only after his death, when the various contours of the role of teacher became familiar to me, could I understand the core of what it was that caused this shame.

It has the same pathetic nature as the teachers who cry at graduation speeches: as vexing as any situation in which the witness is an exogenous element with regard to the chemical process that unfolds. We see and feel the heat of combustion, but are not a part of it. To my adolescent eyes it recalled the afflicted identification an audience feels with a bad actor in a full house. When the actor's good, we identify him with his character, and when he's bad, with his own person. A mechanism fails him, and we're invaded by a feeling of error, almost guilt, like we shouldn't be watching something as intimate as public failure.

It's a distant scene, my father with Armando, because it's

so long ago in time, and because it's malleable, from that distance, in my memory. Now it's flying at me like a magnet and adheres to the memory of my father helping me with my articles and classes. With Armando he was the teacher who taught by example, delighted with his student, and playfully pompous with his disciple. It reminded him of the musician he'd been when he was young: together they rediscovered the stages of secret knowledge he'd already accumulated, leaving what remained of the secret for a hobby, social gatherings, alleviation. Armando had talent, intelligence, aesthetic hunger. He was swift, he composed a personal paideuma: he knew how to insert his own voice into the classics, he played with the rhythm, but he didn't try to hold his own like it was his art form. It was just another fling, and the fire went out within a few months. The scene now establishes itself as true, it takes on its due proportions, and my father returns to solid shape. The teacher who persists, trying to retain the young spirit that slips away, fleeting and diffuse: that's life, that's youth, and the teacher remains behind a little while longer, savoring the last taste of that rare pleasure of the first time.

> *Let me go, I need to leave*
> *I'm going there to search*
> *To laugh as not to cry*
> *I want to watch the sunrise*
> *See the river waters running*
> *Hear the birds singing*
> *I want to be born, I want to live*

Candeia—*"Preciso me encontrar,"* 1976

The Armando who returns to this scene is one who would never die, who leaped from peak to peak, no valleys, no peace:

he was the perpetual sunrise. Not Joaquim Ferreria—he knew the deep valleys, that's true. But he knew the science of re-birth and wasn't afraid of the dark. I think he even had a taste for things foretold. He wouldn't make a good teacher, with that strange taste restored. He, too, needed room to be let go. Not with me. He was a lot of work as a father. Text isn't art, it's something that man does for his fellow man. Words lie and become a part of life, which is why we can't allow ourselves to be swept along by what they steal from music: surrender, in a text, is danger—always doubt when it turns beautiful. Of course, we want to convince and explain, and beauty helps, but it's pernicious because it creates room for confusion.

> *The thing about turning beautiful is yours. I mean, it's some-thing of yours that you're putting in, and it's all wrong. How can I explain? I don't like ugly things, but that's not my point. We have to seek out information, it needs to be liberated, clean. It's about truth and error. Style, fluency, levity: they're foolish ideas from your dearly departed Grandma Ana. We're talking about text and not art: it's much more serious and also more foolish. It's serious because it's not yours, it's nobody's, it's of the world and to the world it will return, shaped with words. But it exists before that. The cell, for example, the mitochon-dria: they're there. It's the same when you're calling a strike: the demonstration of everything wrong with the country, in politics—it's already all there before you do it. Yes, you say, but it's an opinion, or a group resolution, it's not information, but a summons. Look, what do you think will convince people to respond to your plea? Reasoning, exposition. Present to them the things they cannot see but which are already there, not in you, but things in common. Be simple and repeat yourself. Vehemence is situational, not textual.*

> Joaquim Ferreira—*reminder*, circa 1959–60

Joaquim Ferreira wasn't a big reader and his *choro* didn't have lyrics. But he liked listening to samba, was intrigued by the lyrics. My mother warbled as she worked around the house, and sometimes he would correct her on one of the verses. He liked Mario Reis and his tastes suggested he was into bossa nova, but he had a problem with it. Maybe it was a question of class: all those clean-cut boys with their American success. But he was clean-cut too: no drama, all concentration and restraint. Pronouncing each syllable clearly, nothing sentimental, only music. Dona Joana would get a song in her head and sing it all day long, the timbre of her voice fluctuating with her mood. If she messed up her stitching or became displeased with anything, *get that smile outta my way, I wanna come over with my pain* took on a militant melody, with a bellicose tone of defiance. First thing in the morning she was more sensitive to the romance of the world: *I'll have a quail's egg for dinner, it'll get me outta this pickle* became a saccharine lamentation, emerging from a broken heart. Dona Joana wasn't very attentive to words in general, and not only with regard to music. She trailed off in the middle of sentences, got distracted, mixed up names, and was still easily understood by all.

Joaquim Ferreira was the detailed one, an orderly man who had a hard time with any collective, particularly those that contained variables of diverse nature: for example, daily life. A focused subject, perhaps a little too focused. If everyone did his bit the whole world would be better off. It had nothing to do with Germanic selfishness or liberal individualism: doing one's bit meant looking out for each other.

> *I found a kitten in the street and mother let me keep him. He has white and yellow tiger stripes. He stays all day in the cardboard box I lined with cloth. He doesn't eat, doesn't meow, doesn't want milk. He didn't even pee or poop. I think he's going to die.*

His eyes get wide at any little noise. I try to make him happy by petting him, but I think I'm so sad that I only make him scared. I think we're going to die. Guto got here last night, the same day I found the kitten. After Armando died, I knew he was going to be home soon—father said so. Someone called father, he hung up and said to mother: they got Armando, go get Guto's room ready, and then he fell silent. Then he came and I was happy because he was alive and Lígia wasn't going to be an orphan and also because I like him a lot and I thought he was going to die. I took the cat out of the box and put him on my lap, on my chest, to see if he might feel better by listening to the beat of my heart. But it only made him more scared. He took off running and went to hide in a corner and meow. He doesn't want any of the bread or milk I left in a saucer near his cardboard box. I got a postcard from José—he's in London. It was a psychedelic postcard and barely said anything. There was a lot of stuff written in English, and he called me baby. I'm happy Guto's here, but he's so sad. The whole house is weird. It seems like something worse is about to happen. It's better not to die for now, mother needs my help. Hold on a little longer, kitty. He's got quiet over there in his corner. Maybe if I'd left him in the street, the mother would have come back. Lígia doesn't cry much, she's cheerful. Guto still doesn't put her in his lap. I don't know if he's happy to see her. She's so cute. Mother took a photo of her and wanted to send it to Eliana, but we don't know where she is. Dona Esther is coming by all the time to see her grandbaby. She's weird. She was very sad at Armando's burial. All in black, with a veil, she looked like something from the theater, and a little like a turkey buzzard, too. The kitten meows and meows and Lígia cries and mother comes to pick her up. I don't want to pick up the kitten, dumb cat, afraid of everything. Here's your milk, dummy.

When I was little and Armando was already grown up, he taught me how to play hopscotch. We didn't have chalk, so he scraped the ground with a stone, making big squares, for someone his size, and then wrote HEAVEN in big letters, but upside down. I still didn't really know how to read, but I knew that it was upside down and I complained. Armando told me that's how it was supposed to be, because it was only heaven when you got to the top and started to come back. Then José, who was almost never home anymore, he had it out for me, and he came the next day and wrote other words. He wrote them firmly, with some kind of yellowish brown stone. The stone that Armando used was white. José wrote something along the side of every square.

Mother just came into my room. I'm here pretending to study because I don't want to be out there, everything seems bad, Guto's voice is thick and low, mother is letting Lígia stay in here so I can watch her while she makes dinner. Her crib is next to my bed, and she stays in there playing with a little bunny that mother made for her, with long ears for her to suck on. She makes little noises that other babies don't make.

On our hopscotch court, José drew a large ball, like a lake, before number 1, and wrote HELL inside. Next to the first three squares he wrote, INFERNO. Beside four and five, he wrote FLAMES. Next to the sixth he wrote SCORCHED EARTH, and along the seventh and eighth, he wrote VERDANT FIELD + CLOUDS, but upside down, like HEAVEN. I didn't understand the words when I got home and saw them. I had school in the afternoon and my brothers had class in the morning. When I came home and saw all that, those letters that I understood individually, but not how to put them together, I got really mad. I didn't know what he wrote, but it was mine, and he had no right to mess it up. Guto was my friend, and when I got his attention, I asked for him to read it to me. He read it and I didn't understand some of the words, but I understood the sequence and I didn't like it. Guto said that we could erase it *with a broom, but I knew that it wouldn't do any good, it was already marked for good, scraped into the earth, and now that every part had its own name, this was what they'd be called, even if I wrote other names over it and nobody could read the words José had written. The first name was always the right one, I knew that, and Guto thought he could distract me because he didn't want me to be sad, he thought that I was still too small to know about serious things.*

I think it was always a little bit like that. I could count on Guto to protect and help me, but for knowing about serious things in the world, I paid attention to José. He sent me a tape of the Beatles, called me little sister, *told me I'd flip if I were with him in London, he wrote me that I have to hear* Tommy *by The Who, but he didn't send me a tape and I think I still don't have that record. He lives with his friends in a big, old house, he says that it's the best, a superfamily but without the judgment: there's children, babies, music, and everyone laughs and cries and talks and everything's great, nobody polices anybody else, he tells me that I have to get hip to the idea that the world is a lot bigger than Vaz Leme number 7, by a long shot, that medicine is great, it lets you understand your body, see inside it, it saves people and births them from their mothers, but there are other journeys before that, that the world is just starting now, in this precise and exact moment, that medicine and school can wait, and what I need to do is get out, take off, see what's out there, smell the roses because life is short and it's going fast, baby, a lot faster than at Vaz Leme 7, let me tell you. A chill wind is gonna come, the leaves will fall, my dear, and you won't have seen anything, honey, you won't have smelled the scent of poppies at sunrise, shivering to death.*

Sometimes I think just that, my brother: that I'm a little baby girl hidden behind her mother's skirt, a coward who still needs the board that Grandma Ana put over your yellow HELL*—that*

*board that was the bridge to goodness, guarded by good angels
who never slept and who were stronger than the worst HELL.
And I crossed the bridge and then could begin the game: tossing
the stone, hopping through the infernos and flames because the
angels at the bridge that grandma built gave me strength. And
then I get angry about it all, about Vaz Leme and this cat that
won't eat and meows with fear, about my own fear and laziness. Sometimes I pack my backpack, sometimes I write stories
of girls who leave, sometimes I listen to Janis Joplin and cry
by myself, sometimes I kiss Nando and he squeezes my breasts
and feels up my legs and we listen to Janis Joplin together and
I forget about my sadness and I smell the scent of the poppies
at sunrise and I remember the way Armando's hands made me
fly. I used to cross over your hell feeling nice and warm because
Armando held me firmly and made me leap like a ballerina,
before grandma's bridge was ever built, Armando's warm hands
lifted me, I flew and fell into his lap and I was glad there were
infernos and flames and everything else because I liked to fly
with Armando, until my father got home and Armando never
came back and you left and never came back. Once I wanted to
be Rita Lee. Another time I wanted to be in London with you.
But sometimes I think that you're an asshole who got left out
because you're just a nothing, a nobody, zero.*

*Ligía went to sleep, the cat is sniffing at the bread dipped
in milk. Today is Friday. Father got home and supper is almost
ready.*

Jussara—*loose leaf paper*, probably April 1970

I don't remember the cat. I remember very little from those
days. Jussara was studying for her college entrance exams and
was helping out a lot with Lígia. When I'd studied for those
exams in the back room, she was still playing hopscotch on
the front patio. Even after José's words were washed away by

the rain and she'd redrawn the game, Jussara kept the board where it was. Maybe I've confused the cat's cries with Lígia's, and for that reason have a vivid memory of her as forlorn. The whole house was vulnerable and forlorn. In that supper, maybe that's it, there was a confusion that even up to today I attributed to my reserves of hallucinations, at that supper when our father took an eyedropper from his vest pocket and said the cat was still to small to know that its discomfort was caused by hunger, that for this reason Jussara needed to feed it milk from the eyedropper, force it down if she had to. My mother said something about the fish being tender and in my memory it was recorded that they were feeding Lígia with the eyedropper and giving her tender fish, which sounded a little crazy because she was too big to be fed with an eye-dropper and too small to digest fish. My fingers were half-crooked, I was afraid of dropping her on the floor, I preferred not to pick her up. I felt like I had been made permanently dirty, something covered in stench and sweat, it seemed to me that Lígia got upset whenever I came near. My father no longer held evening meetings, he didn't play the flute. He was no longer part of the union, maybe it was shut down by the regime. Sometimes people came over, but it was rare, and I don't think they were his colleagues. He didn't like these visits, and sometimes they were young people, they might have been from the organizations, other times they were shadowy figures whose provenance I couldn't determine. Those were confusing times, every utterance cut short, everyone suspected, I was always half-dirty and disheveled, returning to the home I'd left four years before. I hadn't lived with my parents in the time before I went to prison. A lot of work, studies, marriage, the new house. Eliana pregnant, anyway, maybe some of those people had been guests in the house in that time and it was I who was the stranger there and every-where else. Aside from the deaths of Eliana and Armando, my insomnia and auditory hallucinations made memories of this period dirty and diluted.

The 1970 World Cup, entire series of plays, Jairzinho's joy, Pelé's leap, Tostão's ranking, his hope, the malice of a fakeout, and something free and determined, a group of large, fearless men, this remained with intensity among the fragments in my memory. Today, it makes me happy to remember. Today I understand the sequence of the plays and their link to each game. At the time I was excited, I learned of each pass be-tween black holes. The feeling was too big, too crushingly sad to fit in my chest. And if it didn't work? If the ball didn't make the goal? If they intercepted a pass? If we didn't win? What would become of us? And those big, valiant men? And Brazil, what would become of it? We had a TV, it was small and black and white; I remember the games in color, the tight shorts, and various plays in slo-mo, ultra-slow, centuries, the muscles tensing, the leg turning, the foot catching, the ball fitting perfectly, smacking against it to go flying, traveling, sailing over, spinning with style against a forehead that al-ters its trajectory and sends it flying like a bullet to the goal. An immense joy rings out, my father quiet, staring in that fixed way the stroke had left him, a mask that swallowed hard, his Adam's apple rising and falling and then, after the goal, his shoulders relaxing, his head lowering, his blink delayed. There were other people around, maybe friends of Jussara's and neighbors who didn't have TV. I remember the small chil-dren, and Lígia on my mother's lap. Everyone jumping and shouting, hugging, my ear aching, I stretched my mouth wide to unlock my jaw, I went out to the street and felt the flutter-ing of my heart. Once again, disaster had been avoided. We're

143

not going to die, not now. They're good, they're the best, it's clear and scientific, but that's not enough. Other times we were the best and still lost. Being right or certain never matters: there's disappointments along the way, and others who are certain, something we only perceive later, when everything is over. But it won't be that way this time, I have faith that it won't. We'll save ourselves, I believe in God the father we will. Our Lady the Untier of Knots will light our bath and confuse the spirits of our adversaries. I thought things like that, they lacked any kind of center, I wasn't even thinking, they were phrases that flew through my head, coming from who knows where. I was afraid for the children and for Lígia, for all the women of Brazil, it seemed to me that if we lost the Cup, it would be a truth that lasted forever, an eternal *never again* was at play in that Cup, in the feet of those Brazilian demigods. What insanity was this? Violent, bizarre rationale.

This was how I lived through the conquest of the triple championship and the few other things I clearly remember about 1970, a clarity that is, perhaps, excessive. It's not the games I remember, but individual plays made by specific players, and the feeling of imminent catastrophe that would befall us all in the event of a loss. I don't remember the cops dragging me out of my home, or my arrival to prison. I imagine the cells were down below, because I do recall going upstairs for interrogations. But I think there was sunlight wherever they held us. I remember the sound of the cell door opening, the cold that clutched at my stomach, the desire to vomit. I remember that I didn't talk. In my first few days back at home, I remember the desolation of the house, Lígia's cries, Eliana's chills, and Luiza's voice on the telephone. I don't remember anyone telling me about Armando's death or Dona Esther's later on. I remember Dona Esther whispering in Lígia's ear and the disappointment in her eyes. Today I can't imagine what the day-to-day life at home and at work in the schools must have been like. I know that I resumed my position as principal and teacher before winter vacation began in July. I don't remember who, nor where, nor in what situation, but they told me my file with the Department of Political and Social Order had been pulled and it was clean, there was no impediment.

With everything lumped together, memories and the unremembered, I start to think I got it wrong. Maybe no one has ever considered me a traitor except myself. And something else: I don't remember this having been important in the last twenty years, but it returned with a vengeance in the days after my retirement, as I think about this interview, and as I leaf through old papers and prepare to abandon the house. In any case, if it's still so strong, it can't be a false problem. Yes, the first step over which the others aggregated, forming this calculation that has perturbed me, shaking my mind from the inside, generating friction and infections, blocking vital channels, forcing others to break open, after which things calmed until this violent resurgence at the onset of old age—this first step might have been a misunderstanding. No, misunderstanding is a bad term, it presupposes truth and lies, which might have been different. That, right there, is the truth. It might have been some other way—it always can be. *Now we're getting into what-ifs*, as the commentator on the game put it the other day on the radio.

The term is bad because it doesn't take into account that there was a propitious environment for this kind of calculation to be made. If it weren't for that, things might have been altogether different: Luiza's voice, the doubting eyes I spied, perhaps in error. I never understood, for example, why they let me stay on as principal. Maybe they weren't so organized, or maybe I wasn't so dangerous. It was a fertile time for paranoia in general. Any flap of a butterfly's wings in Japan might have precipitated the formation of this history of betrayal in me.

Brazil: love it or leave it—last one to leave, get the lights. Man is dead, then as now. Vietnam, Albania, the Soviet Union, Mozambique, Mao's Red Book, Guevara dead and mythified, Allende still alive. But this life of buses and bakeries, the life of classrooms and waiting in line, was the same miserable life as always.

> *Ay, ay,*
> *What a thankless life the tailor leads!*
> *When he errs he ruins the fabric*
> *And when he succeeds, the clothes don't please*
> *If it slips, your hand?*
> *I'm cutting the cloth.*
> *And if they're disappointed?*
> *I'm cutting the cloth!*
> *Are you cutting the cloth?*
> *I'm cutting the cloth!*
> *Are you cutting the cloth?*
> *I'm cutting the cloth.*
> *Germano, get lost, before you get tossed.*
> *I'm a novice tailor*
> *and work even for sailors*
> *I only get it right if there's some kind of slight*
> *If God helps with the suit, it turns out a beaut*
> *in the North American system.*
> *I'm a novice tailor.*
> *I just pick up the scissors and start cutting the cloth.*

> Luiz Gonzaga, Miguel Lima, J. Portela
> —*"Cortando pano,"* circa 1950s

Dona Joana sang as she cut. No, we weren't all equals, even if we went arm in arm. Everyone had his own history of cutting the cloth, of flowers and guns and lovers. I don't remember anymore why this mattered. Life was meaningless and I hadn't died for my country, nor for the revolution. I hoped and I don't know what else there was, only the heavy weight on my arms and legs, everything slow and difficult, the ideas of betrayal and death, powerlessness, and barely any rage. It was the bitter taste of defilement and defeat. I, too, would go cutting the cloth, getting rid of Germano, disappointment, God, 'beauts, and the North American system. What I wanted was only to cut and cut and cut, the cloth, anything, whatever, all that mattered was cutting.

I still have one certain memory of 1970. I don't know what made it survive, but it's still there, intact. It almost pains me, it's so alive, and it didn't exist a few days ago. But it came with sound, image, and temperature, it seems like I only understand it now, rather, it's only now that I'm living this long-passed moment. It was recorded and archived before I became aware of its existence. It's nighttime, the women aren't here—maybe they're asleep. We're in the living room, my father and I. We're not wearing jackets, but are dressed for going out. He has on his black coat with the worn elbows, his collar opened in a V. I must be wearing a coat, too, but I feel cold. I'm on the sofa in front of the window to the street. It's dark outside, the air is dry, and occasionally I hear a bus going by in the distance. It must be late. My father is in the armchair, his back to the verandah. He looks at his feet as he talks, sometimes glancing up to face me. Gustavo, he says, Armando reaped the death he sowed. He pauses. He took his mother and sister with him. Silence. I'm uncertain whether he's about to start a new thought or if he wants me to speak.

No, he doesn't: he's stopped to choose his words carefully, he needs to be clear, it's important that I understand. I wait and force myself to pay attention, I'm distracted, maybe tired. He lifts his head and says, "Armando," but then breaks off. He gets up and goes to the window, gazes into the darkness of that night in 1970, when there were still no streetlights on our street. He's wearing slippers and I think about how long I've known those slippers. They were way too big for me. He turns around, leans against the low parapet, crosses his arms over his chest, lifts his shoulders, and looks up at me. It's difficult to tell whether he's emotional or angry. Perhaps he's only being serious. He's the age I am now, an old man. I see an old man. I'd never considered it that way. And, at the same time, here in this room, in this moment, he is my father, the one who knows and transmits. I delay my return to being the child who receives. Armando chose his own path, which wasn't yours. It wasn't Eliana's or his mother's, but he, the son and brother, wanted it that way. He falls silent again. Father, I say, these are difficult times. He hangs his head, smooth hair falling over his forehead. He adjusts his hair and then wraps his hand around his chin, covering his mouth. Standing, leaning, legs crossed. They always are. Times are always difficult. I don't know what he's saying. It's neither consolation nor lament. We hear Lígia's frightened cries, a vigorous fear amid the silence, and then my mother's steps. A prattling, sobs. I have my back to the staircase, but from the sounds and the direction of my father's gaze I perceive my mother coming down the stairs and going into the kitchen to warm the bottle. She must be holding Lígia, because the prattling continues. It's okay, it's okay, it's over, grandma's here, oh!, oh! baby girl, grandma's little girl, sssh, sssh, sssh, bom bom bom. We wait. She takes Lígia back upstairs. You have a family to take care of, he says, mother, sister, and daughter. I close my eyes, runs my hands across my face. The conversation is annoying me, I don't want to listen anymore. He continues: they're three women, your family. I get up and wrap my arms around my body, then rub my hands to get warm and wake myself up. What he's saying sounds like a senile lamentation. Yes, father, they're three strong and healthy women, hard working and understanding, we'll manage, all of us. I turn to put an end to the conversation, go upstairs, get in bed. I stop, turn, and sit on the arm of the sofa. I look at my father and ask with my gaze, what is all this about, anyway? Gustavo, I'm talking to you, I'm trying to tell you something, it's important for you to understand that you weren't supposed to be the one to die, you have your responsibilities, and Armando had his. I start to get an idea of what he means. He's blaming Armando. But why all this now? My father is without strength, white and distant in the dim light of the living room, but he's resolute. He can see I understand and am displeased. Father, no one is supposed to die, you know that. Everything's all wrong, and it's not even over yet. I slouch, I didn't want to talk, I don't want to think, everything's all wrong, why stir things up. Gustavo, he says in a soft voice, it's over now. It ended. Armando went too far, he lost control. He thought he could do it, that he'd find a way, but things got out of control. And now it's over.

That's what I'd tell you, Cecília, if it were possible.

The author wishes to thank

the friends I interviewed and consulted: Dona Cida Castilho Rocha, Maria Lúcia Ovidio, Antonio Perosa, Isaias Pessotti, Ricardo Abramavay, and Maurício Mogilnik (in memory),

Professor Marcos Lorieri, for the story of Benício, told in one of his classes at Pontificia Universidade Católica,

my colleagues and students at Acaia and at Ilha de Vera Cruz.

Special thanks to my friend Francisco Augusto Pontes.

— BEATRIZ BRACHER

New Directions Paperbooks — a partial listing

Javier Marías, Your Face Tomorrow (3 volumes)
Harry Mathews, The Solitary Twin
Bernadette Mayer, Works & Days
Carson McCullers, The Member of the Wedding
Thomas Merton, New Seeds of Contemplation
  The Way of Chuang Tzu
Henri Michaux, A Barbarian in Asia
Dunya Mikhail, The Beekeeper
Henry Miller, The Colossus of Maroussi
  Big Sur & The Oranges of Hieronymus Bosch
Yukio Mishima, Confessions of a Mask
  Death in Midsummer
Eugenio Montale, Selected Poems*
Vladimir Nabokov, Laughter in the Dark
  Nikolai Gogol
  The Real Life of Sebastian Knight
Raduan Nassar, A Cup of Rage
Pablo Neruda, The Captain's Verses*
  Love Poems*
  Residence on
Charles Olson, Selected Writings
George Oppen, New Collected Poems
Wilfred Owen, Collected Poems
Michael Palmer, The Laughter of the Sphinx
Nicanor Parra, Antipoems*
Boris Pasternak, Safe Conduct
Kenneth Patchen
  Memoirs of a Shy Pornographer
Octavio Paz, Poems of Octavio Paz
Victor Pelevin, Omon Ra
Alejandra Pizarnik
  Extracting the Stone of Madness
Ezra Pound, The Cantos
  New Selected Poems and Translations
Raymond Queneau, Exercises in Style
Qian Zhongshu, Fortress Besieged
Raja Rao, Kanthapura
Herbert Read, The Green Child
Kenneth Rexroth, Selected Poems
Keith Ridgway, Hawthorn & Child
Rainer Maria Rilke
  Poems from the Book of Hours
Arthur Rimbaud, Illuminations*
  A Season in Hell and The Drunken Boat*
Guillermo Rosales, The Halfway House
Evelio Rosero, The Armies
Fran Ross, Oreo
Joseph Roth, The Emperor's Tomb
  The Hotel Years

Raymond Roussel, Locus Solus
Ihara Saikaku, The Life of an Amorous Woman
Nathalie Sarraute, Tropisms
Jean-Paul Sartre, Nausea
  The Wall
Delmore Schwartz
  In Dreams Begin Responsibilities
Hasan Shah, The Dancing Girl
W. G. Sebald, The Emigrants
  The Rings of Saturn
  Vertigo
Stevie Smith, Best Poems
Gary Snyder, Turtle Island
Muriel Spark, The Driver's Seat
  The Girls of Slender Means
  Memento Mori
Reiner Stach, Is That Kafka?
Antonio Tabucchi, Pereira Maintains
Junichiro Tanizaki, A Cat, a Man & Two Women
Yoko Tawada, The Emissary
  Memoirs of a Polar Bear
Dylan Thomas, A Child's Christmas in Wales
  Collected Poems
Uwe Timm, The Invention of Curried Sausage
Tomas Tranströmer
  The Great Enigma: New Collected Poems
Leonid Tsypkin, Summer in Baden-Baden
Tu Fu, Selected Poems
Frederic Tuten, The Adventures of Mao
Regina Ullmann, The Country Road
Paul Valéry, Selected Writings
Enrique Vila-Matas, Bartleby & Co.
  Vampire in Love
Elio Vittorini, Conversations in Sicily
Rosmarie Waldrop, Gap Gardening
Robert Walser, The Assistant
  Microscripts
  The Tanners
Eliot Weinberger, The Ghosts of Birds
Nathanael West, The Day of the Locust
  Miss Lonelyhearts
Tennessee Williams, Cat on a Hot Tin Roof
  The Glass Menagerie
  A Streetcar Named Desire
William Carlos Williams, Selected Poems
  Spring and All
Mushtaq Ahmed Yousufi, Mirages of the Mind
Louis Zukofsky, "A"
  Anew

*BILINGUAL EDITION

For a complete listing, request a free catalog from New Directions, 80 8th Avenue, New York, NY 10011 or visit us online at **ndbooks.com**